THE TANGLEWOOD TERROR

Kurtis Scaletta

THE TANGLEWOOD TERROR

ALFRED A. KNOPF 🐎 NEW YORK

THIS IS A BORZOI BOOK PUBLISHED BY ALFRED A. KNOPF

Visit us on the Web! www.randomhouse.com/kids

Educators and librarians, for a variety of teaching tools, visit us at www.randomhouse.com/teachers

Library of Congress Cataloging-in-Publication Data
Scaletta, Kurtis.
The Tanglewood terror / Kurtis Scaletta. — 1st ed.
p. cm.
Summary: When a giant glowing fungus encroaches upon thirteen-year-old Eric's small town, he, his little brother Brian, and a runaway girl try to stop it—and figure out what happened to the Puritan town that had mysteriously disappeared from the same spot.
ISBN 978-0-375-86758-3 (trade) — ISBN 978-0-375-96758-0 (lib. bdg.) —
ISBN 978-0-375-89845-7 (ebook)
[1. Mushrooms—Fiction. 2. Family life—Maine—Fiction. 3. Brothers—Fiction.
4. Runaways—Fiction. 5. Maine—Fiction. 6. Horror stories.] I. Title.
PZ7.S27912Tan 2011
[Fic]—dc22
2010035994

Printed in the United States of America
September 2011
10 9 8 7 6 5 4 3 2 1
First Edition

FOR ANGELA, WHO STANDS UP FOR ANIMALS;
AND FOR BYRON, A FUN GUY.

Chapter 1 THE STRANGE CLEARING

There are just enough woods behind our house to get lost in, and Mom doesn't let Brian go out there by himself. He's nine and I'm thirteen. Until last year she didn't want me in the woods by myself either. Now I'm qualified to be his guide.

Brian goes out by himself sometimes anyway, but that morning she heard him sliding open the back door.

"Take Eric!" she shouted.

I was in the kitchen, reaching for the Cheerios.

"Can you go with him?" she asked, now that she'd already volunteered me.

"I guess so." I shook the box and heard the few remaining O's rattling on the bottom.

"Spend the day with him if you can," she said. "He gets lonely." She grabbed the coffeepot, letting liquid drip and fizzle on the hot plate. She was going to work, even though it was Saturday.

"Come *on!*" Brian shouted.

"Fine!" I shouted back, setting the box down.

Two minutes later I was out on a bug hunt.

It was still dark, and the morning fog made me feel even stiffer and sorer than I did when I woke up. It was warm for October, but the dampness sank into my bones. Some of the lesser aches and pains had faded, but the rest were now more distinct—a shoulder that felt not quite put back into place, and a dull throbbing in my head from an accidental helmet-on-helmet blow. On top of all that, my stomach was growling.

"Why can't you just find bugs in the backyard?" I grumbled.

"I like to look in different places," Brian said. "It's like what Dad says about fishing. You can't overfish in one spot."

The path we were on was one of the better ones, snaking its way south to Boise Township. Birds were skipping around in the branches, trilling and chirping. Michelle can tell you which one is which, but I don't care—I just like the sound of them all going at once. As we came around a curve, a squirrel screeched at us and scrambled off over a rock. I was hungry, tired, and sore, but it was kind of nice being in the woods in the morning.

"Let's look under there," said Brian, pointing at the boulder.

It was about three feet across and two feet wide—bigger than I wanted to deal with—and nestled pretty deep in the mud.

"Does it have to be that one?"

"Why, can't you lift it?"

"Of course I can. I was just . . . Never mind."

I'd brought a garden shovel with me, knowing it might

come in handy. I scraped the mud away from the sides of the stone, then got my fingers under it and gave it a big heave, wrenching the same shoulder that was already throbbing from a rough open-field tackle on Thursday.

The stone was easier to roll over than I'd thought it would be. Two or three grubs were there, waving their disgusting little appendages. I looked away and gagged.

"Stag beetles!" Brian grabbed them up with his bare hand and dropped them into the jar he was carrying. He'd gotten good at identifying bugs, even larval ones like the chubby, shrimplike things that were nothing like the pincer bugs they would turn into—or would have turned into, if they hadn't been somebody's breakfast.

"That's enough, right?" I asked.

Brian nodded, but before we headed back to the trail, he stopped.

"What's over there?" He pointed past some trees.

"What?" I looked but couldn't see anything special. Brian didn't explain. He bounded over the boulder and disappeared behind some bushes.

"Come here!" he hollered. "You got to see this!"

I took a moment to memorize the scene: the big rock I'd just rolled over, the tree right next to it, and the bushes behind it. I didn't think we'd get lost, but it didn't hurt to have a marker or two. Once I had the scene committed to memory, I plunged into the woods after Bri.

I stepped out on a quaking, jumbled layer of rust-red dead boughs. All the trees were down in a ragged circle about ten yards wide. The smell of rotting vegetation was overpowering, even to me—and I'm used to the smells of compost heaps and locker rooms. It looked like a spaceship had landed and crushed everything in its path.

Even spookier was a faint bluish-green light glowing from beneath the dead wood.

"What's that?" Brian asked.

"I don't know." I crouched and peered through the branches. There was a bubbling puddle of neon ooze down there. Maybe the spaceship had left some alien goo behind to infest our planet and turn us all into pod people.

"I'm going to see." He dropped to his knees, set the jar down, and shoved one of the dead branches aside. He tossed one in my direction, sending up a cloud of white dust.

"Be careful," I told him. Even if it wasn't alien ooze, what if it was toxic waste?

He threw a second branch my way, then laughed while I tried to wave away another dust cloud. But he wasn't laughing at me.

"Look!" He pointed.

There was a cluster of mushrooms, and every one of them was lit up like a little blue Christmas tree. Was something spilled on them, or did they just glow like that naturally? I knelt to get a better look.

"Sometimes they turn into monsters," said Brian.

"What?"

"Like in Gninjas," he said. That was a video game he was obsessed with, about gnome ninjas saving the Garden World. "The mushrooms light up, then they turn red. When they turn red you have to smash them before they blow up and turn into monsters."

"Come on, Brian. That's make-believe."

"I *know*," he said. "That's just what they look like."

Even if they didn't turn into monsters, there was something wrong with them.

"Give me your jar," I told him.

"Why?"

"I'm going to take a few mushrooms. I need to show them to someone."

"Who?"

"I don't know yet."

Brian let the bug larvae slide into his hand, stuffed them in his pocket, and gave me the jar.

I knelt down to scoop up a few of the mushrooms with the shovel. I wanted to get some soil, too, so the mushrooms would live for a bit longer. I dug a circle around a few mushrooms, planted the shovel, and levered up the sod. The hardest part was breaking the roots. They were no thicker than threads but tough as steel. They seemed to tug back as I tried to saw through them with the edge of the blade. I worked up a sweat doing it, finally got a shovelful of the mushrooms, put them sideways into the jar, and screwed on the top. I was careful not to touch any in case they were dangerous.

"Are you going to keep those in the house?" Brian asked.

"I guess so, yeah."

"What if they do turn into monsters?"

"They'll be trapped in the jar."

"Oh, yeah." He laughed at the idea.

I was glad to get out of the strange clearing. We found the big rock I'd just rolled over. From that angle it looked like a toppled tombstone, and the damp ground where it used to lie looked like a grave. It put me on edge a little, which is why I nearly jumped out of my skin when a figure leaped out from behind the rock and let loose with a scream that sounded like a dinosaur getting electrocuted. I saw that once on one of Brian's cartoons, so I knew exactly what it sounded like.

The screamer broke into laughter, and I saw that it was only Randy Weaver, one of my teammates. He lived a few miles away in Boise Township. He was wearing running pants and was sopping with sweat so I guessed that he'd been jogging through the woods. He was a real jock.

"You got him good!" said Brian.

"Not you, though. You didn't even flinch." Randy offered him a hand and Brian high-fived it.

"Fine, you startled me," I admitted. "You're just lucky I didn't get you in a piledriver."

"Hey, save that for the Oxen quarterback," said Randy. "Whatcha got? Fireflies?" He pointed at the jar.

I shook my head and passed it over.

"Holy cow," he said. "They look like something out of . . . out of a horror movie or something. Where'd you get them?"

"Right there." I pointed back over my shoulder with my thumb.

"No kidding. Are there more?"

"Lots."

"They're cool. I'm going to take some photos." He took a phone from his pocket and flipped it open. "Hey, show me that piledriver, Undertaker-style." He held up the phone to get the picture.

I picked up Brian, who hollered and flailed while I demonstrated the pro wrestling move, except for the last part, when you're supposed to drive the guy's head into the ground. Even the pro wrestlers don't do that really; it's all make-believe. Randy snapped the picture and gave me a thumbs-up. I set Brian down gently, but he was still mad.

"No picking me up without asking!" he hollered, and ran up the path toward home.

"What's up with him?" Randy wondered.

"Little brothers," I said.

Mom was gone when I got home, and Brian was in his room with the door shut. Arkham Hat Shop blared through the door. That was Dad's old band. They were popular in Boston back before I was born, but they broke up when Dad got married and moved to Maine.

Last winter Dad started hanging around in the basement a lot, strumming on his electric guitar and listening to his band's old CDs. Mom finally asked him if he wanted to give the rock and roll thing another try. She thought he'd get together with some guys on the weekends and jam in the basement, but what Dad did was call up all the other guys from Arkham Hat Shop and talk them into getting the band back together—in Boston. All the other guys still lived there.

"I wish I could explain this to you," he told Brian and me. "I know it sounds selfish of me, running off to chase my dream, but I'm doing it for you guys. I want you to know that it's never too late to follow your own dreams." He looked at me first, really seriously. "That means you should never give up on football, Eric."

"All right," I agreed, but of course I'll have to give up on football by the time I turn his age. Most pro football players retire by that time.

He turned to Brian. "What's your dream?" he asked.

Brian didn't even think about his answer before he blurted it out. "I want pet hedgehogs."

"Sure thing, kid. We'll go get some this weekend."

"Cool!" That was how he got Digger and Starling. He was only eight at the time, and his dream had already come true.

With the curtains pulled in my room, I could still see a faint blue-green shine on the mushrooms. What if there was something seriously wrong in the woods? Maybe there was a chemical spill, or nuclear waste dumped where it shouldn't be. I set the mushrooms on the dresser and watched them for a while, but they didn't do anything interesting other than glow.

If we still had Internet access I could look them up, but Mom got rid of it when Dad left. She said we had to cut expenses. The library was open but there was usually a line to get on the computers. Michelle might know what they were, and I had to go over there anyway to take care of Cassie.

I figured I'd better take Brian with me, since Mom had asked me to spend the day with him. I went and tapped on his door.

"Hey, Bri, want to go to see Cassie?"

He opened the door a crack and looked at me with hurt eyes.

"First say you're sorry. I don't like being picked up."

"I know that now. Sorry. So do you want to go?"

"Can we go to the haunted house after?" There was a haunted house downtown every October, but I wasn't a big fan.

"Maybe tomorrow," I said.

"All right," he agreed.

I glanced at the terrarium, which was a mistake. One of the hedgehogs was still working away at a grub. I would have lost my breakfast, if I'd remembered to eat any.

Chapter 2 THE MYSTERIOUS LIGHT

Tanglewood is built like a spider, with the downtown at the body and a lot of legs spindling off this way and that into the woods. We live at the end of one leg, and Michelle lives at the end of a nearby leg. It's easier to take a shortcut through the woods than walk up one road and down another.

Brian ran on ahead, nudging rocks and logs.

"Looking for more bugs?"

"It doesn't hurt to look," he said.

I had the jar of mushrooms with me. In the light they just looked like ordinary mushrooms, but they had a blue glint when we passed through the shadows of trees.

Michelle is from Boston. She used to be a portrait photographer, but she got tired of taking pictures of people and decided to take pictures of nature instead. She thought she'd run a little farm, because apparently there's always a market for pictures of cows and pigs and horses, but she way underestimated how much work even one animal is, especially when it's a pig. So she settled for one pig and hired me to help out. The pig turned out to be camera-shy and doesn't even pay her own keep. She is cool to have around, though.

Brian and I wedged through some pine boughs and scooted down a steep bank to Michelle's place, which was fenced in but the gate was never locked. She had a big field of weeds, big enough to put a football field, with the house and pigsty on one end and the compost heap on the other. The gate was at the compost heap end.

"Pig poop!" Brian shouted. He was right—that's mostly what the compost heap was made of. We trudged past the heap and through the field to the sty, which was attached to a shed where Cassie slept when it was raining or cold. Now she was basking in the sunlight and lazily cuddling a pink bucket. She got up as soon as she saw us and trotted over.

I scratched her ears, and she made huffy-puffy noises, tilting her head and closing her eyes.

"Can I?" Brian asked.

"Of course."

He reached out and gently stroked the bristly side of her other ear, laughed, and gave it a good rub. Cassie grunted and stepped closer, startling him a little bit.

"It's all right," I told him. "She doesn't bite or anything." Sometimes she snorted and got pig slobber on you, but Brian could learn that the fun way.

"Hey!" I heard Michelle's voice and turned around. She was waving from an upstairs window. "Can you feed her?" she hollered. "I've got a lot going on."

"Yes!" I gave a couple of exaggerated nods, in case she couldn't hear.

"Come see me when you're done!" she shouted, then disappeared from the window.

I set the jar down and headed around front, where I found a fresh bag of garbage from Emily's Café. They save up their food waste for Cassie and drop it off every day. I broke open the bag and filled her food trough. She had her head buried in the mess before the bag was half empty.

Cassie is quick but methodical, first going for the berries, bananas, and apple cores, followed by the half-eaten waffles and pancakes, then turning her snout to the piles of scrambled eggs. She'll even eat leftover pieces of bacon and sausage, which I don't like to think about. The restaurant tries to leave them out, but a little bit always ends up in the bag. If Cassie's still hungry after all that, which she always is, she'll eat the soggy hash browns soaked in ketchup, but not if there are onions and peppers mixed in.

It's kind of fascinating to watch her eat. It's like watching Tom Brady throw a touchdown pass or David Ortiz hit a baseball. She's perfect at her own sport, which is eating.

"Wow," said Brian when Cassie left the sty a few minutes later.

I freshened the water in her water trough and brushed her backside. The only thing left to do was shovel poop.

"Gross," Brian said as I scooped the manure into an old wagon to haul out to the heap.

"It's honest work," I told him, which is what Dad used to say whenever we complained about chores. The truth is that I like doing it. It just feels good to take care of someone. I dragged the wagon across the field to the compost heap. When I got back, Cassie was running alongside the fence, softly booting the bucket like a soccer ball and squealing.

"Is she okay?" Brian asked.

"Yeah, she's just exercising Babe." That's what Michelle called it.

"Babe?" Brian asked.

"The bucket. She thinks of it as her baby. She had a lot of real babies, but they were all taken away from her." Michelle told me once that Cassie used to be a breeding sow and that she'd had eight litters.

"What happened to them?"

"They got turned into bacon. What do you think?"

"Oh." Brian got a sad look on his face. I myself was thinking about not eating bacon anymore, but it's hard to make the connection between a big friendly pig like Cassie and crispy strips of breakfast meat.

I got the jar and went to Michelle's back door, Brian running to catch up. She opened the door before I even had a chance to knock.

"I'm going to be gone for a week," she told me as she let us in, "so you'll have full-time Cassie duty."

"No problem. Where are you going?"

"Baxter to shoot bears. They're most active just before hibernation."

Brian's eyes got wide, so I softly punched him in the shoulder. "She's taking pictures," I told him. "She'd never actually *shoot* a bear."

"No hitting," he muttered.

"Sorry."

Michelle put out a package of cookies, and I grabbed a couple. She poured two cups of milk. Brian dunked his cookie into the milk and held it until it was good and soggy.

"Hey, have you ever seen these?" I pushed the jar across the table. "They look normal now, but they were lit up when I got them. And they were blue instead of yellow."

"Sure I have," she said. "I've seen 'em in blue, green, and orange. It's called fox fire."

"What does it have to do with foxes?" Brian asked.

"Nothing. It means 'fake fire.' I think somebody mispronounced a French word and it stuck. They're not that rare, but they are tough to photograph. The light doesn't come through. Even if you do it with a slow shutter speed, people think you faked it."

"Hm." So they were kind of boring after all.

Michelle must have seen my disappointment and tried to make up for it.

"You know what? I read once that fox fire is where fairies come from."

"Really?" Brian perked up at the mention of fairies.

"Folks used to see the mysterious light shining in the woods and thought that little creatures must be having big parties out there."

"Why didn't they just go see?" I asked her.

"The woods were dark and scary, and since they didn't know what the blue light was, they assumed it was something bad."

"That's, uh . . ." I was going to say "dumb," but I'd done the same thing. I'd thought the glow was alien ooze or nuclear waste, and I was afraid to take a closer look until Brian made me. I resolved to be more reasonable from now on.

Michelle saw Brian scowling. "I don't mean Tinker Bell," she said. "Their fairies were little demons."

"Cool," he said.

Chapter 3 THE TOWN THAT DISAPPEARED

The next day there was a ragged line of mushrooms strewn across our back lawn, petering out before they reached the back steps. With their cone-shaped caps tilting this way and that, they looked like skinny gnomes on the march. It was like they'd followed us.

No, I told myself. We must have tracked spores on our shoes and clothes. I remembered the plume of white dust and shuddered. Those spores had been all over me. In any case, it was scientific. It was creepy and weird but scientific.

The Patriots were playing the four o'clock game on TV, and I got bored during the one o'clock game. I went outside and took the mushroomy trail all the way to the clearing. The mushrooms had spread to the edges of the clearing, right up to the stone I'd turned over yesterday. They looked dull and yellow in the sunlight, but I could still see a blue-green glow deep in the shadows of fallen branches.

I didn't like them, even if Michelle said they were normal.

I kicked at some mushrooms as I strode back through

16

the yard. I knocked a few caps off, but they were tougher than they looked.

"Can we go to the haunted house now?" Brian asked when I got in.

"Um . . ." I'd forgotten all about it. "Not now. The Patriots game is about to start."

"You promised!" he said, which wasn't true. I said *maybe* we would go. I meant no.

"Oh, take him," said Mom, who was on her way downstairs with a basket of laundry. "He never gets to do anything *he* wants to do."

"But the game is about to start," I said. Besides that, did she think that yesterday's bug hunt was my idea?

"Well, the sooner you go, the sooner you can get back and watch it."

So we got on our bikes and headed toward downtown but barely got to the end of the street before Allan waved us down. Allan had just moved to Tanglewood that summer. He was about halfway between Brian and me in age and always wanted to hang out with us.

"Want to play HORSE?" he asked us. He had a basketball hoop nailed over the garage door and spent a lot of time practicing by himself. I'd played a couple of games with him, but his driveway was slanted and I got tired of uphill layups really fast.

"We can't right now," I told him.

"We're going to the haunted house!" Brian added.

"Ooh, a haunted house. Can I come?" he asked.

"All right, but hurry up," I said. He ran inside with his ball, and Brian and I were left standing out there for ten minutes while he got permission. I hoped the Broncos won the coin toss, because I'd miss at least the first drive.

"Let's race," I said when he was finally out with his bike. Before either he or Brian could say no, I took off and pedaled like mad. I got pretty winded halfway but still beat them both by five minutes.

When I caught sight of the orange banner with ghoulish black letters, I felt a little knot in my stomach. It's a pretty plain-looking building, but it is really old. There used to be a colonial village called Keatston where Tanglewood is now, and that was the Keatston Meetinghouse. It's a museum most of the year, but they turn it into a haunted house every October to raise money. I felt the knot in my stomach for two reasons. One was what happened to me there once, and the other was what happened to the village of Keatston.

Brian and Allan were still pedaling up Keatston Street. The main road through town was named for that village. I decided to go ahead and buy tickets for all of us to speed things up.

"We close at four," the woman at the front door told me. She wouldn't take my money. I glanced at my watch and saw it was three-fifty.

"Come on. One last group?"

"Well, make it quick. We all want to see the game."

I paid for three tickets and turned back to see what Brian and Allan were doing. Their bikes were locked up, but they were talking to someone.

"Hey, Parrish!" he shouted, and waved. It was Tom. He was also on the football team, and one of my oldest friends.

"Hey, Chains!" I went closer so we didn't have to keep shouting at each other. His last name is Beauchesne, pronounced "Bo-chains," so everyone calls him Chains.

"Your brother was telling me about your pig pal," he said.

"I have a job taking care of her," I told him.

"I guess you got a date to the fall dance all lined up too."

"Yeah, very funny," I said. "We better get going." I pointed at the haunted house with my thumb. "I want to get home to watch the game."

"Yeah, I'm watching it at Papa's Pizza. Don't get too scared in the haunted house, Parrish."

Allan snickered.

"Later, Chains," I said, pushing Brian and Allan toward the door of the haunted house before Tom could say another word.

Four years ago Dad took Tom and me to the haunted house. Brian was still too young for it. They had a witch that year—this woman with stringy hair and big clusters of warts on her face. I saw her in the shadows up ahead, shuffling across the corridor and disappearing into hidden doorways in the maze we had to walk through. There were also skeletons and spiders and everything else, but I barely noticed them, because I knew that sooner or later the witch was going to jump out and shriek at us. I looked up ahead and saw a vertical line of daylight, which I guessed was the exit door. Here it comes, I thought—the last big fright before we leave. I hung back so Tom would get the worst of it. That was when I felt something in my hair and took a swipe at it. My hand met another hand—a bony hand with long, misshapen nails. I heard a low, throaty cackle and felt a blast of warm breath that smelled of old meat. . . .

And I started bawling. I couldn't help it. I was shrieking and crying, and Dad had to carry me out like a colicky baby. Tom told kids at school, and life was hard for a while. I still felt a little knot of shame whenever I went to the haunted house, like someone there might recognize me and remember.

"It's okay to be scared," I told Brian and Allan.

"Hey, I'm not scared!" said Allan.

"But it's okay if you are," I said.

We went in and saw silhouettes of skeletal trees cut out of black poster board. Some years the haunted house was a walk through a creepy mansion, and sometimes it was a cave. This year it was a path through the woods.

The first display was three stuffed bears—not teddy bears, but taxidermy of real bears—propped up in chairs, licking their plates. A child's blue smock and buckled shoes were at the center of the table, so it wasn't porridge on those plates. After that there was a headless horseman, who had a jack-o'-lantern for a head but no horse.

"I don't get this one," Allan said at the next display. There was a black curtain draped from the ceiling. In front there was just a sign: WELCOME TO KEATSTON.

"It's the town that disappeared over two hundred years ago," Brian told him. "It burned down or something."

"What do you mean, *or something?*"

"It means the buildings besides this one were all reduced to splinters and everyone was gone," I said.

"But there weren't any ashes," Brian added in a whisper.

Allan looked at me, and I nodded. "Nobody knows exactly what happened."

"You're both making it up."

"Well, it's not like I saw it for myself, but that's what everyone says," I told him. "They have this old picture showing the town burning down, and people running around and screaming." I looked for it, hoping to see the picture we always saw on school trips. It wasn't in its usual spot. Some things are too scary for a haunted house. "And there's writing on it that says something about a fire. . . ."

" 'The devil's fire may burn again,' " Brian quoted. " 'God's wrath will purify the earth. The seeds of redemption are in the people.' "

"Yeah, the devil's fire. You remembered all that?"

"Our class was here last month," Brian said. "I memorized it."

Allan looked at the sign again with new appreciation.

"Let's move on," I said. I was all for respecting the past, but there was a game on.

We moved on to see a graveyard. A couple of zombies climbed out of their graves, but it wasn't very convincing. Past the graveyard was a witch, smiling and cackling as she poked at a pot of goop, stirring up clouds of smoke. It wasn't the same witch as the one who used to be there, and frankly, the new one wasn't fit to carry her broomstick.

• • •

We got home during halftime. The Pats were up by ten points. I was sorry I'd missed it but glad they were ahead. Brian went outside to do whatever, and I told him not to get lost in the woods.

As it turned out, I'd missed the good part of the game. The Broncos tied it up in the second half and won in overtime. As soon as the game was over, I went out back and finished stomping down the mushrooms in the yard. I blamed them for the Pats losing. It wasn't rational, but I didn't want to be rational.

"Whatcha doin'?" Brian asked, coming out of the woods.

"Nothing. You shouldn't be out here this late."

"It's not that late."

"It's nearly dark."

There was a high-pitched sound coming from the woods, and Brian wheeled around to see what it was. Against the blue-green night rose a fan-shaped cloud that looked like a giant hand coming to smash the house. The cloud got higher and wider, spreading out and dissipating into the darkness.

"Wow," said Brian. "It's like a million bats."

That might not have even been an exaggeration. I knew that a lot of bats lived in the woods, but I'd never seen so many at once. Maybe they were migrating, but I wasn't sure if bats did that. Either way, seeing that added to my feeling that things were going really wrong with the world.

Mom still wasn't home. She'd left a note on the fridge that there was an emergency at Alden, the all-girls school where she worked, and that I ought to make dinner. She always had the freezer stocked with pizzas, fish sticks, and other easy dinners. She trusted me to put something in the oven without burning the house down. I heated up fried chicken from a box and some frozen peas. Yeah, I don't want to show off or anything, but I can also work the microwave.

We ate in the family room, watching a DVD about dinosaurs and robots warring in various historical eras. We'd already seen it a dozen times.

"Peas are gross." Brian pushed his to the side of the plate, some diving off the edge and onto the floor like tiny green lemmings.

"Don't eat them, then," I said. "I don't care."

He started peeling the crunchy skin off a drumstick with his fingers.

"Hey, that's the best part," I said.

"It's greasy."

"That's why it's good."

"It's disgusting." He finished shelling the leg and nibbled on the meat. Meanwhile, the dinosaurs on TV got some help from Leonardo da Vinci, who showed them how to build a flying machine to defeat the robots.

"I don't think this is accurate," I told Brian, who rolled his eyes at me. I wanted to make sure he didn't get really messed-up ideas about world history.

Mom finally got home at about eleven and went straight to the family room, found the remote, and turned on the TV. Brian had been playing a video game until two minutes before. He'd run upstairs the second he heard her car in the driveway.

She flipped through the channels until she found the news on channel 8.

"Did you make supper?"

"There's chicken and peas in the fridge."

"Great." She went off to the kitchen, fixed herself a plate, and came back. We sat through some of the usual stuff, Mom munching quietly.

"This is it." Mom pointed at the screen with her fork.

There was a fuzzy photograph of a girl with curly dark hair and big Harry Potter–style glasses. It looked like it was taken with a webcam. It wasn't the usual newscaster guy talking, though. It was just the same robotic voice that read off weather warnings.

"Boise Township, Maine: An alert has been issued for fourteen-year-old Amanda Morris. Amanda was last seen at approximately two-thirty p.m. on Sunday afternoon at Alden Academy. She is believed to have run away." They gave a number to call in case you saw her and wanted to squeal. So that's where Mom had been all day—trying to track down a missing student.

"I hope she's okay," I said.

"Me too."

"You hope who's okay?" Brian asked, coming into the room. He'd put on pajamas and mussed his hair. He rubbed his eyes for effect, to make sure Mom would think he'd been in bed and asleep.

"Nobody," Mom said. "I don't hope anybody's okay." I'm sure she didn't mean it to come out the way it did.

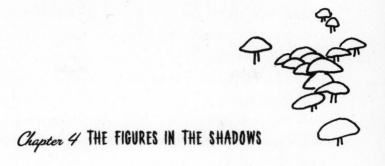

Chapter 4 THE FIGURES IN THE SHADOWS

The mushrooms had already grown back in the yard Monday morning, thicker and meaner than yesterday. I was really beginning to hate the sight of them. I went out the front door so I wouldn't have to walk through them.

Brian ran to catch up.

"You're supposed to wait for me," he said.

"Oh, yeah."

"I can go to school by myself, but Mom gets mad at me if she finds out because I'm not supposed to."

"Sorry, bud. Anyway, you don't have to worry. Mom left early." Before I even got up, that was. I'd found half a pot of coffee still cooling on the hot plate and a note on the fridge.

"Do you have practice today?" Brian asked.

"Yep."

"Drat. I don't want to go to the stupid library." He kicked at a pebble and sent it flying. I made a mental note to teach him placekicking one of these days.

"What's wrong with the library?"

"It's boring," he said.

"I know, but I thought you liked it." I knew he liked

25

the Japanese comic books you read backward, and he liked playing on the computer. He could even watch movies on one of the TVs with headphones plugged in. It was both the public library and the school library, so it had lots more than educational films.

"I'm just sick of it," he said. Mom made him hang out at the library until I was done with football. When I had away games, he had to wait for her to get home from work.

"I'm sorry." I guess it would be boring after a while. "Can you go to a friend's house or something? Like go shoot hoops with Allan."

"I don't know," he said. "Maybe."

I waited around after science class that afternoon until the other students left.

"Yes, Eric?" Ms. Weller asked me as the last kid finally got out the door.

"Um, I found some mushrooms in the woods that light up," I told her. I'd left the jar at home because the mushrooms had withered and faded. "I'm kind of worried."

"It's called bioluminescence," she said. "It's nothing to worry about. A lot of living things emit light, from fungi and bacteria to insects and fish."

"I'm not worried about the light," I told her. Michelle had already set me straight on that. "There were some dead trees, though. I thought the mushrooms might have killed them."

"Most forest fungi consume wood that is already dead or dying. The trees aren't dead because of the mushrooms; the mushrooms are there because of the dead trees."

"Oh." I wasn't convinced, but she was a science teacher.

"You know, you could do a science discovery project about it," she said. We could do one of those a quarter for extra credit. Kids brought in dead caterpillars and broken geodes, stuff like that. "Just remember that you can't just bring something in. You also have to research it."

"Yeah, I know." Last year I'd brought in Dad's tuning fork but couldn't explain how it worked. "Where do I start?"

"Look up the honey fungus," she said. "And get your sample soon, because the first cold snap will wipe out the mushrooms. None of them survive the first frost."

"Got it." Honey fungus: that was easy to remember. I didn't bother to write it down. The bit about the first frost was good news, too.

"The Internet is a starting point, not the only source of information!" she called after me on my way out.

I knew teachers had to say that, but seriously—didn't the Internet know everything by now?

"One more game," Coach said, holding up an index finger in case we needed a visual. "One more win, and you'll be perfect. Do you know how many pro teams in history have had perfect seasons?"

"Just the '72 Dolphins," I said. The Pats should have, a few years ago, but laid a big egg in the Super Bowl.

"Exactly," he said, pointing at me with the same index finger. "Who won the Super Bowl the following year?"

I shrugged.

"Exactly again. Nobody cares about that one. It was

just another Super Bowl. There's only one goal bigger than winning a championship, and that's to be a champion among champions." He got a look of bliss on his face. He looked like Cassie when she was getting her ears scratched.

"This school has only had two winning seasons before this one, and you've already given them a third," he said. "I was student-teaching for the last one. You guys weren't even born yet. That's how long ago it was. We've *never* won a championship. You guys can give the school its first. But you also have the biggest dream of all, right within your grasp: a perfect season. The town will remember a championship for years to come, but if you have a perfect season, the whole league will remember. The Oxen will remember. The Green Wave will remember. The Minutemen will remember." He went through all our opponents, telling us they'd each remember our perfect season. "You can do it," he said. "All you have to do is beat the Oxen again. On your home turf."

The gravity of the situation hit us. We'd already beaten the Oxen once, on their turf in Blue River. Randy had returned the second-half kickoff for a touchdown, and that was the only score for either team. The Oxen protested that the one touchdown shouldn't count because they didn't have all their defenders on the field. The refs said since they kicked it off, it was their own fault. It didn't feel like a legitimate win, but it was better than losing.

The Oxen had a really good defense. Better than our defense, I thought. If it wasn't for that lucky TD, we probably would have lost that game in overtime.

"Do you know what oxen are?" Tom asked, breaking the silence.

"Cattle," Randy said.

"*Castrated* cattle," Tom corrected him. "We're playing a bunch of castrated cows, guys."

The serious mood turned into laughter.

"We can beat a bunch of castrated cows!" Tom said. Some of the guys shouted in agreement, and most of them clapped. Even the eighth graders joined in.

"All right, that's enough of that," Coach said. "Let's practice."

We broke off into groups and did our drills.

I'm one of four seventh graders on a team that's mostly eighth graders, the others being Tom and Randy and Will. When Coach picked me and Tom and Will, he said it was because we were "filled out" enough to play. "Filled out" means big and fat.

Randy wasn't big at all. He was small, but quick and tough. He could run right through defenses and shed tacklers twice his size. He scored most of our touchdowns and was the main reason we were undefeated. Randy was already getting pressured by prep school coaches and thinking about whether he'd go to USC or Texas for college. He even had a nickname picked out: the Dream. "I'm going to change my name to Dream Weaver," he said one time in the locker room after a big game. "People always talk about living the dream; I'm going to *be* the dream." Nobody called him that yet, but sometimes it takes a while for a nickname to stick.

I was the only seventh grader on defense, mostly playing middle linebacker or strong side linebacker. We blitzed practically every down, which some of the other coaches thought was cheating, because we were good at it. "No reason to stop doing it if it works," Coach would say to other coaches. We were only allowed to blitz with five guys, anyway—four linemen and one linebacker. I was always that blitzing linebacker, so I got a lot of tackles. I'm fast for a fat guy, and I don't have any fear when it comes to throwing myself at someone and knocking him down.

"Hey, Parrish, I need to talk to you," Coach said, coming over to me while I beat the stuffing out of a tackling dummy. I knew what it was about.

"Coach, that helmet play was a total accident. It was a clean tackle. He tilted his head." My helmet had crashed into another kid's helmet during our last game, knocking both of us a little senseless.

"That's not how the official saw it," he reminded me. "They saw it as a fifteen-yard penalty and threw you out of the game."

"I know," I said. Just thinking about it got my heart racing. Unsportsmanlike conduct, they called it. It was totally unfair. "He didn't see what really happened."

"Just don't give them anything to see wrong on Thursday, all right?"

"I'll try," I told him, but I couldn't control what the refs thought they saw.

"Trying is for people who expect to fail," he said.

"Right. I'll do it. I mean, I won't do it."

"You won't do what?"

"I won't give them anything to see wrong."

"Good boy." He slapped me on the back. "This game is as much about discipline as it is about talent. Now go get that dummy."

I did, imagining it was that stupid referee from the last game. I didn't need blind refs ruining everything. I don't have a nickname picked out, and no prep schools are talking to me, but I have big plans too.

I couldn't find Brian at the library. He must have gone to Allan's. I did see an open computer and took it.

"We close in twenty minutes," a librarian dude told me, tapping his watch. "Just FYI."

"Okay." That was plenty of time to look up the honey fungus and whether or not bats migrate like geese. I'd forgotten to ask my teacher about that.

I checked my Facebook messages first. I had a couple of friend requests from kids at school and said okay to them. Dad had written on my wall: "I heard your team is in the championship game! Way to go, big guy! Can't wait to talk this weekend." He'd posted that on Friday but hadn't called over the weekend.

"I also saw that I was tagged in a new photo. I found it on Randy's page—the one of me holding Brian upside down, **pretending** I was about to ram his head into the ground. The comments were full of OMGs and LOLs. Randy didn't bother to explain we'd been fooling around. I started to write a comment but didn't post it. It might just make things worse.

I'd wasted too much time and only had a few seconds to scan the honey fungus article on Wikipedia. The main thing I learned was that the fungus was like an apple tree, and the mushrooms were the apples. The tree part was underground. So we hadn't scattered the spores. It was one big fungus, reaching out for us belowground. I pictured it creeping toward us beneath the earth, stretching its giant fingers, getting ready to reach up and grab—

"Five minutes," the library guy said. "I need to ask you to shut down."

"Fine." I shut down the computer. I had to go take care of Cassie anyway.

It was dark by the time I got there, but over by the pen I could see a few figures in the shadows. When I got two or three steps closer, I saw that it was my teammates: Tom, Will, and Randy "the Dream" Weaver.

"Hey!" I shouted, waving, wondering what they were doing there. They turned and looked at me, and I got a sense that something besides pig poop stank about the whole scene.

Then I saw what was going on: Tom had Babe and was waving it around in front of the pig. She grunted and tried to paw her way through the fence but couldn't. He started pounding on the bucket like a kettledrum and singing. Cassie ran back and forth along the fence, making little whimpering noises.

I dropped my backpack and tossed my equipment bag to the side.

"Come on, Tom," I told him, trying to keep my voice even. "Give her back the pail."

"What's the big deal?"

"She . . . It's like her baby," I explained. I felt my fists clenching but forced my hands open and tried to smile. "She thinks of it like a baby. It's kind of silly, but she gets really upset when people take the bucket away from her." But he must have known that, I realized. Why else would he do it?

"It's not a baby, Eric." He showed it to me. "See?"

"Yeah, but it's still hers." I grabbed at it, but he pulled it away and tossed it to Randy.

Will laughed. "Keep-away from Eric!" he yelled.

I took a step toward Randy, but Will got in the way, bowing his arms, getting into his guard position. His footing has never been that good, and I knew the mud wouldn't give him good traction. I get by better offensive linemen all the time. I gave him a well-placed shove and he slipped and fell.

"What was that for?" he asked.

"Shut up, Will. What do you think?" I stepped over him and made another move at Randy. This time Tom came in to block.

"You don't have to be a jerk about this," he said. "It's a bucket, Eric."

"It's like her baby," I told him. "She's had at least sixty piglets, Tom. Sixty babies, and every one was taken away from her. They're all bacon now. Every last one of them. So if she thinks the bucket is her baby, who are you guys to take it away from her?"

"It's a bucket," he said slowly, like he was trying to calm down a three-year-old.

I shoved him aside, and Randy took off running. I gave chase, Tom lumbering behind me and Will behind him. Michelle has a lot of land, so Randy had plenty of room to juke and deke and sprint and do shimmies and all the show-offy stuff he did when he was running against lousy defenses. I got winded right away, and I knew I'd never catch up. But I also knew that the little hill Randy was headed for was the compost heap. I knew that he'd want to be the king of that castle. A guy like Randy can't resist the chance to be king of something.

It was a bad, bad decision. One second he was ten yards ahead of me, and the next second he was knee-deep in pig poop. I caught him with my left arm, hauling him to the ground. The bucket slipped out of his hand and bounced away.

"Fumble!" I shouted, nearly hysterical with a sense of victory. I grabbed it and ran back to the pen, blowing right past Will and Tom. I gave the bucket to Cassie, who grunted with relief and carried it back to the far side of her pen. She started sniffing at it, making sure it was okay.

"The ball is recovered by Parrish and taken ALL! THE! WAY!" I shouted, doing a victory dance and punching at the air. I finally looked back at Tom and Will, who had struck-dumb expressions on their faces and were staring at Randy, who was rolling on the ground and crying, his leg bent the wrong way at the knee.

Chapter 5 A PECULIAR SILENCE

I ran home through the woods and into the alien blue-green light of our backyard. The mushrooms had splayed out across the lawn and were now in full glow.

I banged in through the family room. Brian was on the Wii.

"Is Mom home?"

"No. She's still at work." He paused the game and looked at me. "What's going on?"

"Nothing." I sank into a chair. "I thought you went to Allan's."

"He didn't want me to come over."

"Really?" That didn't sound like Allan.

"You weren't here and Mom wasn't here, but that's not my fault. How come you're all out of breath?"

"Nobody said it was your fault, and I ran home because it was so late."

I couldn't calm down. My heart was beating at double speed, and I was hot and sweaty. I expected police cars to come screeching down the street after me. I'd assaulted a kid and left the scene of the crime. The first part was an accident, and I only left because Tom had screamed at me to leave—and he'd had his phone out to call 911—but the cops might see things differently.

"You stink," said Brian.

"You're one to talk." Brian had worked himself up into a sweat playing his game, and he wasn't a world champion bather to begin with.

The telephone rang. That was it. They were coming for me.

"You answer," I told Brian.

"What's going on?" he asked again. The phone kept ringing. "Are you in trouble?"

"Just answer it."

He did. "Hello? Okay. It's for you." He handed me the phone.

"Thanks. You're a big help." I took the phone.

"This is Eric Parrish," I said.

"Eric? I need you to make dinner again." It was Mom.

"We, uh . . . There's kind of something you need to know, Mom."

"What?"

"I broke a kid's leg, Mom."

"At football practice?"

"No, it was after practice. It was in a fight. Mom, I think I'm in a lot of trouble." I saw Brian's eyes get big and round.

"Eric, this will have to wait until I get home. Just make dinner for you and Brian and don't get into any *more* trouble, all right?"

"Sure, but I think the police might come."

"Then call me back when they do."

"Mom, you better come home. This is kind of a big deal." If the police did come, I wanted somebody to be here besides me and Brian.

"So is this, Eric. This one is life or death, understand?"

I imagined some girl lying on the ground, turning white as other girls panicked. But what could Mom do? She wasn't a paramedic. Then I remembered the missing girl.

"Understood," I said.

"If the police come, don't say anything. You have the right to remain silent, remember that."

"Yeah, I know." Did she think I'd never seen a cop show?

"Make dinner for you and Brian. I'll be home soon. Sorry, this is just . . . this is really serious, too. We have to find Amanda." She hung up.

The police didn't come screeching into the driveway. I made a frozen pizza. Brian played his video game. I was missing *Monday Night Football* but didn't care. I didn't even know who was playing.

The phone rang again. Brian's Gninja was searching the field for coins so he could advance to the next level, so I answered.

"This is Eric Parrish," I said.

"Eric." This time it was Will. His voice was low, kind of breathy. "Randy's hurt pretty bad," he said.

"He . . . I was just trying to get the . . . I thought we were just . . ." Every sentence died. I didn't want to say anything that would make it sound like it was my fault. It wasn't. Maybe it wasn't their fault, either, but it sure wasn't mine.

"I just thought you'd want to know," he said.

"I didn't," I said.

He clicked off the line. Maybe what I'd said came out wrong. I didn't mean that I didn't want to hear how Randy was doing. I meant that I didn't want to hear that he was hurt pretty bad. I thought about calling back to explain, but the phone rang again.

"This is Eric Parrish," I said. Every time the phone rang, I thought it would be the police and I had to sound official.

It was Mom again.

"Do you want to tell me what happened?"

I did, walking to the kitchen so Brian couldn't hear. I told her everything. Even the part about Cassie's piglets getting taken away from her and made into bacon, because you needed to know that to know why it was a big deal to get her bucket back.

"Eric, we've talked about this before. Just because you're big doesn't mean you can—"

"But they started it this time."

"It doesn't matter who started it," she said.

"I'm sorry."

"I don't think you can apologize your way out of this one," she said.

By morning it looked like our house had vomited up fungus, spewing it from the back door across the porch, down the steps, and into the yard, spattering into the neighbors' yards. It looked a lot like I felt, actually.

The mushrooms were even thicker in the woods, climbing the tree trunks and crawling along the branches. There was a peculiar silence in the woods. It was late in the season for bugs, and maybe the squirrels were hibernating and the birds had all gone south for the winter, but it was as quiet as a cold winter day with newly fallen snow. It was lifeless. Which was also how I felt.

When I got to Michelle's, I saw the papers from my notebook scattered across the field. Did Tom and Will do that while waiting for the ambulance or after Randy was rushed off to the hospital? I ran around and gathered them up. They were easy to see in the dim light, the perfect rectangles of white standing out against the dark grass. The only one I couldn't find was the one with my notes from the library.

I found my textbooks in Cassie's food trough, but fortunately she hadn't eaten them, even though she hadn't been fed last night. I took them out and tried to shake off the spatters of swill, then fed and watered Cassie. When I reached out to pet her, she snorted and backed up, her eyes wide open. She'd never done that before.

I got work gloves and a shovel out of the shed and cleaned the corner where Cassie does her business. When I rolled the wagon across the field, I noticed something black against the brown, barely visible except for a glimmer of smudged yellow. I knew what it was even before I lifted it off the pile and shook it out. It was my football jersey. The rest of my uniform and pads were also thrown onto the heap.

I started to pick them out, but by the time I found the left cleat, which was buried especially deep, I figured it wasn't worth it. I threw the whole stinking mess in a garbage can by the shed and went to school.

That morning at school was rough. I had the feeling everyone was looking at me and whispering about me, which they probably were. If it had been two other kids at the school who got in a fight and one of them busted the other guy's leg, I'd talk about it. I hid behind books and pretended to take furious notes in every class so I wouldn't have to make eye contact with anyone. Randy and I were in all the same classes, but he wasn't in any of them that morning.

I usually sat with the team at lunch, but that didn't seem like a good idea anymore. I carried my tray past tables full of kids staring at me, nobody sliding over or saying, "Hey, Eric, right here." Well, that was my own fault for not having friends outside the team.

I ended up at a table of sixth graders, and they didn't strike me as the cooler sixth graders. They looked back at me in shock. A popular football player like me was not supposed to sit with them. I realized that Allan from down the street was there. I'd never even noticed him in the halls. I didn't know he was in sixth grade. I thought he was in fifth grade, tops.

"Hey," I told him. He looked down at his food and didn't say anything back.

As bad as the morning was, the afternoon was ten times worse.

The science teacher asked me if I'd researched the mushrooms for my oral report, and I told her I had but I'd lost the notes. I didn't say why, but everyone was looking at me like they knew it was connected to everything else, and they were right. I also didn't have the sample to pass around, because even though mushrooms were all over my life like— well, like a fungus—they weren't my number one problem anymore, and I'd forgotten to harvest some new ones.

Then there was a surprise school assembly instead of last period. Everybody was muttering and whispering to each other, wondering what it was about. I myself thought it might have to do with the missing girl from Alden Academy—it's the kind of thing that kids start rumors about. There was a computer hooked up to a projector on a cart, so whatever it was, it was going to involve multimedia.

Principal Dahl coughed into the microphone, causing a squeal of static over the PA. Ms. Brookings, the guidance counselor, stood next to him, looking grim. Now I knew it was serious. The last time they had a surprise assembly with Ms. Brookings, she told us a girl named Gail Hendrickson had leukemia.

"Okay," Principal Dahl said after he got the microphone figured out. "We're meeting today to talk about an incident that took place . . . It was not on school grounds but involved several students here, so . . ." He isn't great at finishing his sentences. "To help facilitate this conversation, we're . . ." He looked back at Ms. Brookings, saw she was there, and handed her the microphone.

"Thank YOU, Mr. DAHL," said Ms. Brookings. She

has a way of overemphasizing certain words. She's also big on exaggerated facial expressions. In the last assembly, she talked about "GRIEVING" and made a sad face like she was talking to preschoolers who wouldn't know what that was.

"I wonder," she said now, making a stagey puzzled look, one outstretched finger to her lips. "I WONDER if someone can TELL me . . . what is a BULLY?" I felt a silent groan course through the auditorium. That's what we were having an emergency assembly for, to talk about bullying? We thought we'd left all that behind us when we got out of grade school.

"Well?" Ms. Brookings shrugged dramatically, shaking her head. "Does anybody KNOW what a BULLY is?"

A girl in front finally raised her hand.

"YES?" The counselor hustled over to hand her the microphone.

"It's somebody who beats up on smaller kids?"

"Okay, okay, yes. A bully is someone who 'beats up' on people 'smaller' than themselves." Ms. Brookings used her fingers for quote marks. "That's good. But what else might a bully do?" She browbeat the kids in the front row until they mentioned name-calling or playing mean tricks or posting junk on someone's Facebook wall. I remembered the picture Randy tagged me in. Did that count? I didn't know.

After all that, she went over to the cart and clicked a button. A cartoon came up with animals who wore baggy jeans and flip-flops and said "Yo, homey" at one another. We'd seen the exact same movie in second grade. I wasn't pro-bully or anything, but the whole thing was dumb. It's not like mean kids don't know they're being mean and will be better after watching a cartoon.

While the cartoon was playing, I saw Randy coming in on crutches. He sat right in front, and the guidance counselor knelt down and whispered to him, nodding with exaggerated empathy when he whispered back.

I got a sick feeling in my stomach, realizing what was going on. The incident that Principal Dahl was talking about—the one that happened off school grounds—was what happened with me and Randy. But they thought Randy was the victim and I was the bully. I could see why they might think that. I mean, Randy is smaller than me, and I did break his leg, but that wasn't the whole story. I almost jumped up to explain myself, but nobody had actually singled me out, so I stayed quiet.

Chapter 6 THE NAMELESS HORSEMAN

I decided to skip football practice. I really wasn't in the mood to talk to my teammates. And besides that, I was probably going to get kicked off the team for wiping out our biggest star a few days before the championship. Brian wasn't at the library, so I went straight to Michelle's.

Cassie was sprawled out on a pile of hay, dozing peacefully, last night's trauma apparently forgotten. She still had food and water from this morning, but I topped off both, then brushed her down on the side I could get at. I didn't need to shovel again so soon, so I swept up some of the dropped goop beneath her trough and carried it to the compost heap.

There were a few dozen mushroom caps dotting the heap. They were the biggest I'd seen yet, and they gave off a blue-green shimmer even in the sunlight. Manure must be a mushroom paradise. I flung the new stuff on the heap and headed back to the sty, putting the wagon and the brush away. Everything seemed to be okay. Wait, where was Babe?

I panicked for a second until I saw it in the corner of the sty. There was something else there, just over the fence—a white garbage bag stuffed full of something. It couldn't have been there this morning. I would have seen it.

It must be food for Cassie, I thought. Even though the restaurant always leaves their scraps around front, not in the sty. I went closer and saw "PIG BOY" written on the side with a bright blue Sharpie. Did somebody from the team leave it there?

I opened it, expecting something awful, and saw black polyester and a flash of yellow. I reached in and pulled out my jersey. It was my whole uniform, washed and folded. There was my number, 97, bright and yellow. The pads were there and everything.

Had Michelle come home, found it in the garbage, and cleaned it for me? I banged on the door, but there was no answer.

I took the shortcut home through the woods, which were still spooky quiet. I realized that the fungus had probably scared all the animals away, just like the cloud of bats I'd seen soaring away two nights ago. The squirrels and rabbits must have gone deeper into the woods to get away, and the birds probably went south. Or maybe the animals weren't scared of the fungus itself. Maybe they knew the woods were dying.

The Wikipedia article said the honey fungus mostly feeds on dead wood, but these trees were alive, at least for now. The branches were drooping and eventually might turn black and fall down like the trees Brian and I had seen the other day. What if the fungus ate its way through trees until it killed the entire forest? I imagined the mushrooms creeping all the way to Baxter State Park, making their way down the Appalachians, and moving west across prairies and deserts and mountains until the entire continent was nothing but fungus. That first frost was way past due and couldn't get here soon enough.

Our next-door neighbor Mr. Davis was in the backyard with a snow shovel, trying to scoop up the mushrooms and toss them back into the woods, but it wasn't going very well. He had to really put his shoulder into it and kick at the back of the shovel to help the blade cut through the roots.

On the other side, Ms. Fisher's Jack Russell terrier was yipping and yapping at the mushrooms, running up and down along the chain-link fence. He finally let loose with a yellow stream at one of the denser patches. Go for it, Sparky, I thought. If those mushrooms were as electric as they looked, his name would suddenly be perfect.

The mushrooms wrapped around both sides of our house, and I followed them to see how far. They'd pushed their way into the front yard but petered out before they reached the sidewalk.

When I looked up, I saw Dad's car in the driveway, a U-Haul trailer latched to the back.

I went inside and found the basement door ajar. I stood on the top step for a bit, listening. Dad was strumming on a hollow-body electric guitar that wasn't plugged into anything and singing my favorite song of his, which isn't an Arkham Hat Shop song or even really by him but one he used to play for me when I was a little kid. It's about a nameless horseman riding through the valley, having all these adventures. "Who can the brave young horseman be?" the song asks, but you never find out the answer. Dad also played a song about an octopus and some others I forget, but the one about the horseman was my favorite.

As a little kid, I thought he'd made all those songs up himself. I got into a huge argument with my kindergarten teacher about "Puff the Magic Dragon." I told her my dad made up that song, and she asked me if his name was Peter, Paul, or Mary.

I waited for Dad to finish, then went down the steps. Brian was sitting next to him, listening. Dad's little practice area is at the west end of the house, the side facing the woods. There were a few dots of bright green on the wall behind them.

"Hey," I said.

"Hey back at you." He strummed once more, good and hard so the strings rang out for a long time. "I guess I should finish hauling stuff in." He put the guitar gently on its stand and came over to give me a hug, squashing my nose with his shoulder.

"You came home, huh?"

"For a while. Your mother says everything is nuts up here."

"It is nuts," I agreed.

"So I'm here to de-nuts-ify it, if I can. Put my job on hold, postponed a couple of gigs."

"Sorry." I was the reason Mom called Dad. I knew that. She must have done it after I'd gone to bed.

"Hey, I told you all, call if you need me. Your mom called, and here I am. I came straight home, just like I said I would."

"How long are you staying?"

"I don't know. At least until they find that girl, so your mom isn't working twenty-four-seven."

"What are you going to do while you're here?" I was wondering if he'd try to work out of the home or something.

"I don't know," he admitted. "Try to help with things, I guess."

"Did you see the mushrooms?" I asked them, pointing at the wall.

"Huh?" He wheeled around and looked. "I'll have to do something about those." He might have been talking about a leaky faucet or a loose doorknob—something he could put off for a few days, or forever.

"They spread really fast," I told him. "They've already taken over the lawn."

"Yeah, I noticed that. Crazy." He started up the stairs without giving them another look. I wished he thought it was more urgent. Maybe he didn't care because he thought he'd head back to Boston in a few days, leaving us to deal with our crazy fungus.

I helped him carry everything else in. There wasn't that much, just his clothes and his laptop and a few other things. He'd only needed the trailer so his guitars wouldn't get smashed up in the backseat.

"So—I hear you're in a spot of trouble," he said as he dropped the last box in the foyer.

"I guess so. I broke a guy's leg." I tried to explain what

had happened, but every time I talked about those guys taking Cassie's bucket, it sounded less like a good reason for a fight. "It was an accident," I said at last.

"Did you tell him you were sorry?"

"No," I admitted.

"That's okay. I think it's better this way, legally. You should probably avoid talking to him until this is all settled."

"Oh." That didn't make sense to me, but Dad did work at a law firm now and probably knew what he was talking about.

"We'll get through this," he said. "Anyway, I have to get the trailer to Millinocket by seven. Can you make dinner?"

"Sure thing."

"Thanks, bro."

A few minutes later he was gone.

Mom called just after he left.

"Dad's here," I told her.

"Already? I didn't think he'd get here today. Well, I'm glad he did. I think it's going to be a late night for me. I'm glad you boys aren't alone."

I didn't bother telling her we were.

"Any luck finding that girl?" I asked.

"We don't have a lot to go on," she admitted. "She just disappeared. But we're talking to everybody in case somebody knows something."

"She'll be fine," I said.

"You don't know that, Eric."

"No, I guess not."

"If you or Brian ever does something like this . . ." She trailed off. "Don't. That's all. I'll see you later." She clicked off.

I wanted to get some fresh mushrooms before it got dark. I emptied the jar and dug up some new ones from the backyard, sawing the edge of the shovel against the tough roots to sever them. I slid the mushrooms sideways into the jar, replaced the cap, and brought the jar back to my room.

"Why do you keep bringing those inside?" Brian stood in my doorway, looking at me accusingly.

"I'm doing a science project on them."

"Why don't you do your science project on hedgehogs? You could bring in Digger or Starling and feed her a bug."

"Maybe next time." I'm sure grossing out the class would be a great way to win back my popularity.

"Is Dad moving back for good?" he asked me.

"Probably not," I said. "He said just until they find that runaway girl." I realized that Mom might not have told Brian about Amanda, but he knew what I was talking about. Everybody in town knew about her.

"Oh." He turned around and went back to his own room, half slamming the door.

I put some potpies in the oven and did homework at the kitchen table while I waited for them to bake. I could have cooked them in the microwave, but I didn't like how soggy and white the crust was when I cooked them that way.

I decided to re-create my science notes so I could give my oral report the next day. I got a notebook and wrote down everything I remembered.

1. **Honey fungus.**

I'd written down the scientific name for it—carefully, so it was spelled right—but that page was gone, so I'd have to call it the honey fungus. The mushrooms sure didn't smell like honey, and I was willing to bet they didn't taste like honey, so they probably got the name from their color in daylight.

2. **All one big thing.**

The mushrooms were all connected, underground, connected by those cords. So it was one big organism, and it could get even bigger. Wikipedia said there was one in Oregon that spread out over a mile in every direction.

3. **Really old.**

The same fungus in Oregon was at least a thousand years old. I didn't know how they knew that, but they did. So these things could be alive for a very long time.

4. **Bioluminous?**

I couldn't remember the exact word my teacher used. I couldn't find the reason they lit up in the article, either. It just said they lit up "in the right conditions."

5. _____ **core.**

I couldn't remember the word, but the fungus had a kind of heart. Everything grew out from there.

It wasn't much information, but it was good stuff. An ancient, giant underground fungus that could light up when it wanted to—that sounded like a sci-fi movie, but it was real. Unless somebody hacked the Wikipedia article just to mess with my head.

Chapter 7 THE INTRUDER

I wrote it all down, neatly enough to hand in, and took the notebook up to my room. I put it in my book bag and went to grab the mushroom jar so I wouldn't forget. It was gone.

"Brian, did you borrow my mushrooms?" I yelled down the hall. He didn't answer.

I went to his room and tapped on the door.

I could hear him moving around, but he still didn't answer. I opened the door and saw him shoving something into the top drawer of the bureau.

He looked at me with wide eyes. He looked guilty, then angry.

"I didn't say you could come in!"

"You didn't say I couldn't."

"Leave me alone."

He tried to slam the door on me, but I wedged my foot into the frame to brace myself and used my whole forearm to block the door.

"What's going on?"

"Nothing. Leave me alone!" He put all his weight into

the door, and I went on holding it open. He grunted and strained, but it was no use.

"Whatcha got in the drawer there, Bri?"

"Nothing."

"It's not my mushroom jar?"

"No!"

"So it's okay if I take a look?" I pushed the door open wider and squeezed past Brian into the room. He was still leaning into it with every ounce of his scrawny frame. When I let go, the door suddenly swung away from him. He stumbled into it.

"I'm telling Mom!"

"What, that you're a klutz?"

I reached for the drawer, and Brian threw himself on my back, wrapped his arm around my neck, and drove his chin into my shoulder blade. It hurt like crazy, and I could barely breathe. Brian had never wrestled, but he must have learned some dirty tricks from somebody. We both fell back onto the bed, me squashing him. The bedsprings squealed under our combined weight.

"Geppupame," he said.

"Geppupame?"

"Geppupame."

"Is that like a country in South America?"

"Moe. Geppupame."

"A rare tropical fish?"

"I said GET OFF OF ME!" He wrenched one of his arms free and pushed, then started punching me.

"Oh! Get off of you. Of course I will. . . ." I shifted my weight so he could breathe, but not enough so he could get up. "If you let me see what's in the drawer."

"NO!"

"What's the big deal?" I was only teasing him at first, but I was starting to seriously wonder what was in the drawer. "Do you have a gun?" I asked him.

"Don't be stupid."

"What then. Drugs?"

"I said. Don't. Be. *Stupid*." He emphasized the last word with a sudden surge of effort to free himself, but I was built like a linebacker and he was built like a wimpy little brother. It was futile.

"Did you steal something? Is that it? You shoplifted a video game, didn't you?"

"No!"

"Oh, I know! One of those grown-up comic books that Mom won't let you buy."

"Shut up!" He turned red, and I was sure I'd guessed right.

"That's it, isn't it! I want to see it." I got up and opened the drawer before he could even react, and started riffling through it for contraband. There were no comics, no weapons, and no narcotics. Not even mushrooms. Just random stuff—his SpongeBob wallet, a Celtics keychain I didn't know he had, some stones he'd found, a souvenir coin from Boston with the Old State House on one side and Paul Revere on the other, his only necktie rumpled beyond usefulness, and a few Arkham Hat Shop CDs.

I picked up a carving I'd never seen before, a colonial man about six inches tall, with a funny hat pulled way down over his brow. He was holding a misshapen ball and was crouched down—looking a bit like the old Patriots logo, actually.

"Did you get this in Boston, or where?" I asked. Brian might have gotten it at one of those little kiosks with cheap stuff for tourists. Not that this looked cheap. It looked old and handmade, but there are machine-made things that look old and handmade.

Brian swore at me.

"Where did you get it?" I asked him again. "It's neat."

"I found it in the woods."

"Is this what you were trying to hide?" I twisted around and saw him sitting on the bed, his face sulky and sore. He didn't answer.

When I turned back, I noticed the terrarium on top of the bureau. Either Digger or Starling was cowering in the back corner, scrunched up into a ball. The other one was hiding.

So that's who I was. Somebody who scared hedgehogs for no reason.

"Sorry," I told the hedgehog. Then I turned to Brian. "Sorry," I told him. "I needed to make sure you weren't doing anything, you know, that I needed to know about." I put the funny little man back into the drawer and shut it.

I heard the oven beeping downstairs. I didn't know how long it had been going off.

"Dinner is ready," I said, and left. Brian slammed the

door good and hard behind me, calling me a bully and a jerk and a bunch of other words. I went downstairs and ate my own potpie, which was burned. Half an hour later, I ate his.

When I went upstairs, the mushroom jar was where I'd left it. Either Brian had put it back or I'd somehow overlooked it earlier.

That night I lay there for a while, awake, with mushroom light breaking through the window.

I didn't know why I'd been so mean to Brian. It didn't feel that bad at the time, but when I played it back in my head, it didn't look good.

I needed to get my mind on something else.

So I played out how things might go if I apologized to Randy. What if I ignored Dad's advice and walked up to the team table at lunch, told Randy I was sorry, and sat down? The other guys would push over and make room for me, maybe somebody would crack a joke, and we'd all laugh. I'd sign Randy's cast, then we'd all talk about the championship game and how we'd beat the stuffing out of those Blue River Oxen.

The game would be a blowout. Better yet, a tight game with an inspiring finish. The Oxen would have a five-point lead and the ball, the clock would be ticking down. All they would need to do is run out the clock, but Randy would be on the sideline, swinging around on his crutches, hollering encouragement to everyone. "Live the dream!" he'd shout. Everyone would stand up and shout out the Owls cheer: "Who's going to win? Whoo? Whoo?"

The Oxen would snap the ball. I'd storm through their tackles, drop the quarterback, force a fumble, pick up the ball, and gallop into the end zone. The buzzer would sound, and the Owls would have won! My teammates would crowd around to heave me up, but I'd point them to Randy. It'd be him we'd pick up and carry off the field.

Sometimes when I can't sleep, I imagine my whole football career, from the University of Maine Black Bears to the Patriots to the Hall of Fame. That night I punched the pillow, turned over, and began again at square one, where I made up with Randy. If I didn't do that, the rest of it couldn't happen.

I got up before dawn, knowing sleep would never come. I rummaged through the Pig Boy bag and moved the uniform to my sports bag, since I'd need it for practice after I apologized to Randy. It looked like everything was there except my helmet, which I always left in the equipment room. But wait—my cleats were also gone. I'd thrown them in the garbage along with everything else, but they weren't here. I'd have to go back to Michelle's house to get them.

Dad was up already, making toast. I grabbed a soda from the fridge.

"You're drinking Coke for breakfast?" Dad asked.

"I guess so." I cracked it open and took a swig. "How come you're up already?"

"I'm used to it. My job in Boston starts at seven, and I have to commute."

"Oh, yeah." Dad's day job was doing computer stuff for a

law firm. He lived in the city and worked in a suburb, which is the opposite of what most people do. When Brian and I visited him there, we all slept on the floor in the middle of the efficiency apartment. It was like camping out, except for the cars going by all night. "I thought maybe the mushroom light bothered you."

"Nah," he said. "There's a neon sign outside my apartment window in Boston, so it kind of reminds me of home." His toast popped up. "Want this batch? I can make more."

"Yeah, that would be awesome." I buttered it and peanut-buttered it and jellied it.

"Can you walk Brian to school? I'm going to go early."

"Of course," he said. "I got nothing else to do."

"We're also low on lots of stuff," I told him.

"No problem. I can go grocery shopping."

"But, uh, I'm not eating pork anymore," I told him, deciding then and there that I wasn't. "So no bacon or anything. Not for me, anyway."

"What about beef?"

"Beef is fine," I said. I didn't know any cows.

After slamming down my toast and soda, I headed through the tunnel of green-blue light to Michelle's house to find my cleats. Halfway there I could hear Cassie snorting and squealing, obviously upset. I couldn't believe those guys were back. Even if they were mad at me, what did Cassie ever do to them? I took off running and stumbled over some tree roots but managed to regain my balance before I went facedown in the mushrooms. I stopped as soon as I got to the fence instead of running down to the gate. I wanted to see what was going on.

There was a teenager-sized person in the shadows, pinned in the corner by Cassie, who was standing her ground and shrieking. Good for her. The intruder couldn't have been Tom or Will—he wasn't big enough—but it might have been one of the smaller players. Whoever it was, I could take him, but he had something in his hand that was hard to make out in the darkness. It might have been some kind of weapon. I didn't want him to see me until I knew what he had.

Cassie's pen was connected to the shed so she could get in out of the cold. The only door was through the sty, but there was a window on the other side, about five feet off the ground. The fence was chain-link, and not a high-security thing. I dropped my backpack and gym bag and climbed to the top and leaped to the roof of the shed two feet away. I landed with a dull thud, which the intruder probably heard, but I didn't think he could see me. I lay there for a few minutes, looking out at the field—which had become dotted by mushrooms—before I crawled to the edge, reached down, and pushed the top pane open. It slid easily and almost noiselessly, a little squeak of wood against wood.

The window was really close to the roof. I wormed my way in, feetfirst, nearly getting Winnie-the-Poohed when I was halfway through, but gravity did its thing and I came crashing down into the pile of piggy-smelling hay where Cassie sleeps sometimes. Something smelled terrible—it was even worse than the usual pigsty smell—making me gag. I pulled my shirt up to cover my mouth and nose, then found and flipped the two light switches. The overhead light came on in the shed, and the floodlight outside filled the sty with brightness. I looked out the door and saw a girl standing there, still cornered by Cassie. She was holding Cassie's brush in one hand and looked terrified. I recognized her. It was the runaway girl.

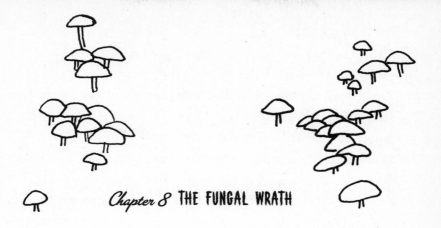

Chapter 8 THE FUNGAL WRATH

I couldn't remember her last name, but I knew her first name: Amanda.

"Finally," she said. "Someone's here." Her voice was frayed, and she sounded close to tears. Her hair was standing up all over, and she looked rumpled and scared.

Cassie came over and bumped her head against my leg, nearly knocking me flat. "It's okay," I told her, reaching down to scratch her ears. She calmed down.

"What's going on?" I asked Amanda. My tired brain couldn't come up with any explanation for a runaway from Mom's school winding up in Cassie's sty. I'd have been less surprised to see my football coach in one of Brian's video games.

"One of the neighbors left a pumpkin on the porch, with a note saying it was one more than they needed for jack-o'-lanterns, and that Cassie might like it. I guessed that Cassie was the pig, so I—"

"You gave her an entire pumpkin?"

"Yeah."

"She can't eat that much at once."

"I figured that out when it all came out the other end half an hour later."

"Michelle calls that the squash squirts."

"Ugh. I tried to clean her, and she went crazy. I've heard that pigs can really hurt people, so I froze and waited for her to calm down, but she didn't, and . . ." She stopped, caught her breath. "I think it was because she had an upset tummy."

"Did you pick up her bucket?"

"Yeah, I filled it with hot soapy water to scrub her down. I must have dropped it." She looked around and found Babe behind her. She tossed it over to me. I shook it out, spattering my jeans. Cassie nudged me in the leg with her head, grunting impatiently.

"I need to rinse this off," I told her. Cassie gave me a particularly determined butt, nearly knocking me over. I got the hose and washed Babe, and soon Cassie was in her hay, cooing at Babe. She needed a bath, too, but it would have to wait. She'd had a long night.

After I retrieved my stuff from behind the fence, we sat in Michelle's living room, which Mandy—that was what most people called her, she said—was actually living in. There was a wad of blankets on the couch, a pile of clothes on a chair, and a plate with a crust of sandwich and an apple core on the coffee table.

"Broke in and made yourself at home, huh?"

"Yeah," she admitted, picking up the blanket so I could sit at the opposite end of the couch. "Except I didn't break anything. I found a key."

"The one in the shed?" Michelle keeps one on a nail, high above the door in the shed. You would never see it unless you knew it was there.

"Yeah. I read this book about a master thief once. He almost never had to pick locks or shatter windows. He was always finding keys buried in the garden under a gnome or tied to a string in a mailbox. It only ever took him a couple of minutes, but it took me two hours. Not that I'm a master thief or even aspire to be one, but I needed a place to stay and something to eat, and neither a hotel nor a restaurant was going to work."

"How did you know Michelle was gone?"

"Um . . . there was mail in the mailbox and no car in the driveway?"

She'd made herself small on the couch, her feet tucked under her sideways, the blanket pulled up over her. She didn't look like a master thief. She looked like a kid up past her bedtime.

"Your parents are probably freaking out," I said.

"I called them and told them I was okay."

"Really?" My mom hadn't mentioned that, but it wasn't like she was giving me daily updates. Mandy might be telling the truth. She was still causing *my* mom to freak out, of course.

"Really," she said. "I even let my father yell at me for, like, half an hour."

"You weren't worried about them tracking you down through your phone?"

"I have ways of doing things," she said. "They think I

called from a landline in Madison, and since my big sister is a student there, they're probably sure that she's hiding me. It's a huge fringe benefit if they get on her case."

I heard my school counselor's voice in my head. "What do you do when you WITNESS any kind of CRIME?" she'd ask. And the right answer would be to call the cops, even if someone borrowed a pen and kept it by mistake. The specifics didn't matter to her, but they did to me.

I imagined it as penalties assessed one after another by a football referee. Illegal infraction of Michelle's house, go back five yards. Trying to take care of Cassie, maybe move up five yards. Making my mom's life difficult, go back another fifteen yards with a loss of down.

"Why did you run away from the school?" I asked. Maybe that would be the deciding factor.

"How did you know I ran away from a *school?*" she asked.

"You were on TV," I told her. I decided to leave my mom out of it for now.

"Oh, right. Well, I didn't really run away. I just left for a few days. I'll go back when I'm done."

"Done with what?"

"I wanted to see something with my own eyes."

"A pig with the squash squirts?"

She laughed, then leaned forward and whispered, even though we were alone, "Have you noticed there are glowing mushrooms in the woods?"

"Of course."

"Do you know what they are?"

"They're called honey fungus. I researched them for school."

"That's what they want you to think." She grabbed her phone off the coffee table and tapped the screen a bunch of times, then showed it to me. She'd brought up a picture of mushrooms. "*This* is honey fungus," she said.

"And those mushrooms look like the ones in the woods."

"The ones in the woods are bluer and pointier. You'll also notice that the ones in that picture have a ring around the stem. Ours don't. I'll show you *our* mushrooms." Her fingers danced across the screen again, and she showed me another picture of mushrooms. This one was an illustration, not a photo. The mushrooms were bluer and more cone-shaped than the mushrooms in the first image.

"Okay, those do look more like the ones growing outside," I admitted.

"They look *exactly* like the ones outside. I wanted to see them for myself and make sure, and now I am sure. They're the same mushrooms."

"Glowing mushrooms are glowing mushrooms. What difference does it make?" Michelle said she'd seen all kinds and colors of glowing mushrooms.

"Let me zoom out." She tapped the screen a few times, then handed me the phone. "This is what we're dealing with."

I had to scroll up and down to see the entire picture. In the background you could see houses smashed to smithereens. I tapped down and saw a massive tangle of branches and limbs that had almost taken on the shape of a monster. Some of the limbs looked more like tentacles, and mushrooms were erupting all over the creature's body. A man lay on the ground, either dead or badly hurt. Another man waved a pitchfork at the thing, but my money was on the monster.

At the bottom, it said:

Next month: **THE FUNGAL WRATH!**
A new story by Maxwell Bailey

"This is from a comic book or something," I told her.

"It's from a pulp magazine called *Weird Tales* in June 1933. The story never appeared. Nobody knows for sure if Bailey ever finished it, but the picture's famous. I recognized those mushrooms immediately."

"So what are you telling me—that our mushrooms are going to turn into that thing?"

"I don't know. That's what I need to find out."

She took the phone back again and put it to sleep, flipping its case closed. There was a vampire dude on the front.

"You like that guy? Edward?" I asked. That explained a lot. If she thought vampires were cool, she might think all kinds of monsters were cool.

"Please," she said. "It's Lestat. He doesn't *sparkle*."

It was all the same to me. If I'm going to read a book, it needs to be about real people and real things, not vampires.

"There's no such thing as a mushroom monster, or whatever that thing is," I told her.

"How do you know?"

"Because it's ridiculous. We'd know if there was."

"There's a lot we don't know," she said. "Do you think scientists have discovered and documented every single species of mushroom?"

"Probably."

"Not even close," she said. "I read that they've documented less than a quarter of the world's fungi, so there."

"Really?"

"Yes. There might be one extraordinary species of fungus that's capable of things we never imagined."

"What are you going to do to it if there is?" I asked her. "Spray it with Tinactin?"

"I don't know," she admitted. "I need more evidence first. That's why I'm here."

"How did you even know about the mushrooms?" I asked. Alden was miles from here.

"There's this Internet message board for fans of old sci-fi and horror stories. This guy Dreamweaver—that's what he calls himself—he posted a photo and said, 'Hey, don't these mushrooms look like the ones in Max Bailey's picture?' And I said, 'Yeah, they look like the ones in "The Fungal Wrath" because they're the same mushrooms.' So I asked him where he took the picture, and he said that it was near Tanglewood, Maine. And I was like, Whoa, I'm a few miles from Tanglewood, Maine. . . ."

I was only half listening, thinking about the guy calling himself Dreamweaver who lived near here and who'd taken a picture of the mushrooms with his cell phone.

". . . and there was no way I could do all of that at the school, because I'm not even supposed to have Internet access, and they try to control you twenty-four-seven. Okay, maybe that's the *real* reason I left. I've been thinking about it since the day I got there, but this was what I really needed—a mission."

She realized I was tuning her out. "You think I'm crazy, don't you?"

"I don't know. I mean, I don't like the mushrooms either, but I don't think the fungus is going to rise up out of the earth and eat the town."

She burrowed under the blanket. "I feel dumb for even mentioning it," she said.

"Ah, don't feel dumb," I told her. "People believe all kinds of stupid stuff."

"Gee, thanks."

"I didn't mean you were stupid," I told the mound under the blanket.

"And after I washed your football uniform," it said.

"Oh, that was you?"

"I saw you throw it out. I hate football but I felt bad for you. Besides, you're a good pig-sitter."

"Thanks." I wondered if she'd seen the incident with Randy as well, and how much of it she'd seen.

"No problem." She finally poked her head out from under the blanket. "Anytime."

"So did you, uh, see my cleats?"

"Yeah, they were pretty nasty, and I didn't want to throw them in the washer, so . . ."

"You left them in the garbage?"

"No. I put them on the bench in the shed, so you'd find them."

I remembered that first big whiff of stink after I squeezed through the window.

"Great." I glanced at the clock. School would start in twenty minutes. I'd left the mushroom jar at home, but I could run home and still get back in time for school.

"I better go," I told her, "and, um . . . so should you."

If I turned Mandy in, Mom wouldn't have to deal with her being missing, and that meant Dad would go back to Boston. He'd said so himself. Brian would be heartbroken.

So Mandy got a bad call in her favor. I wasn't going to turn her in. But I wasn't going to let her run amok, either.

"This is my boss's house," I added. "She's my friend, too. I don't feel right about letting you stay here."

"Fine," she said.

"I'm serious. I'll tell the cops." I watched her closely. If she had seen what had happened with Randy, and seen it well enough to know I was guilty, she could blackmail me.

She didn't let on either way. She had a good game face.

"Don't worry about me," she said.

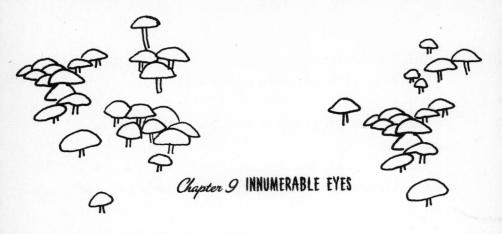

Chapter 9 INNUMERABLE EYES

I ran through the woods, my bags bouncing against my knees, one stinky cleat in either hand.

"Hey, who's that?" Dad hollered from upstairs when I slid open the back door and hurried through the family room.

"It's me!" I hollered back. I took the basement steps two at a time and washed the bottoms of the cleats in the laundry sink, swiping at them with a brush Brian uses to clean the hedgehog terrarium. The cleats were still a little bit stinky and a lot wet, but at least I could wear them to practice without half the team passing out.

When I was done, I noticed Dad's books lined up on shelves made of boards and cinder blocks. He'd never taken them to Boston. They were all out of order, so I hoped that I could find the book I was looking for, if it was even there.

It was. *The Collected Stories of Maxwell Bailey,* in paperback. The cover image was of a forest with innumerable eyes among the trees. It was hard to tell if there were things hidden there or if the trees themselves could see, but either way the effect was creepy. The cover bragged that the book included "Twenty-four color plates of illustrations," so I flipped through to see them. The mushroom monster was in there, sure enough. The caption said it was possibly his most famous illustration, even though the story had never been published, or maybe *because* it had never been published.

I realized I hadn't even flipped on the light to the basement. There was enough light from the mushrooms to read by. They now covered the floor and all four walls. I felt like I'd realized a dozen cockroaches were crawling all over me, and I even did a little dance to shake them off of me before I ran back upstairs to grab the jar.

I still got to school a few minutes early. I staked out my place in homeroom, opened my book, and started reading the introduction. Max Bailey was an only child, grew up in Boston, moved to Maine, and attended Bowdoin College but was expelled for unknown reasons.

Randy was barely in the door before a girl offered to carry his stuff. He'd become a girl magnet like never before, a combination of superstar and vulnerable puppy they couldn't resist.

I read about how Bailey became an illustrator for a newspaper in Portland and wrote stories in his spare time. He got married and had a daughter named Howard—that must have been a mistake in the book—but his wife died during childbirth. He went into a deep depression.

Randy paused at the front of the class and looked at me.

Bailey became fascinated by newspaper articles about unusual phenomena, and he kept folders full of clippings. His short stories took a turn toward the dark and fantastic.

Randy hobbled by me, taking his time. "That book is awesome," he muttered in a low voice as he passed. I nodded, but he didn't even see it. He was already sitting down, talking to a girl. He didn't say another word to me for the entire class.

He found me in the hall later. Dad had said I shouldn't talk to him, but I couldn't help it if he tried to talk to me. The bell was about to ring, and everyone else was in class.

"So how long have you been reading Max Bailey?" he asked.

"For a while," I said vaguely. "My dad has all kinds of cool books."

"I should come check it out. What else are you into?"

I thought hard, trying to remember some of my dad's other books so Randy wouldn't know I was a poser.

"Um . . . Lovecraft?" Dad has a bunch by that guy, and the name stuck in my head.

"Yeah, he's the best, but Bailey's great too. I didn't know you were into that stuff."

"Me neither," I said. "I mean, I didn't know you were." The bell rang. "We're late."

He nodded at his crutches. "I can be a little late. Nobody's going to give me a hard time."

"Hey, I'm sorry about that."

"Me too, man. Hey, I want you to know, I don't kick puppies or set cats on fire or anything. I didn't know all that stuff about that pig and her babies, and now I'm sorry I went along with it."

"Same here."

"We were just kidding around. We didn't even do it to mess with the pig. We did it to mess with *you*. It was Tom's idea."

"Never mind. I guess you got the worst of it."

"So are you playing tomorrow?"

"If they want me to."

"Of course they want you to."

"Tom and Will and those guys—"

"Just Tom and Will and me," he said. "Nobody else even knows."

"Huh?" Everybody'd been talking about me, though. They'd been whispering and pointing. At least I thought they were. I tried to run through the highlight reel in my head. Did I just see kids yakking at each other like always and assume the worst?

"Tom said we should stick together, like teammates do," said Randy. I wondered if Tom felt like it was partly his fault, which it was.

The late bell rang.

"Go ahead," I told Randy. Our next class was together—most of our classes were. "I'll need a tardy slip from the office."

"I'll say you were helping me," he said. "I'll say I fell down or something."

"Cool." We headed to class. Randy was pretty good with the crutches already, but it was slow going.

I couldn't believe I was off the hook so completely, even though I didn't think I'd done anything wrong in the first place. Just yesterday the situation looked hopeless.

"Hey, what about that school assembly?" I asked him before we went in. "Why did the school counselor say all that stuff about bullying?"

"Um . . . I heard some guys dumped a sixth grader in a garbage can. His mom went ballistic and called the school."

"Oh."

"Hey, one more thing," he whispered. "This thing is our secret, right?"

"You mean about Cassie?"

"No, I mean me being a sci-fi geek." I could tell he was dead serious. "I have an image to protect, man."

"You got it, Dreamweaver."

I told Ms. Weller I could go ahead with my oral report. I had one notebook page of notes and a jar of mushrooms. I was all set.

"Eric has volunteered to be the next presenter on scientific discovery," she told the class, followed by some blah blah blah about how the world is chock-full of science for us to discover. "Eric is going to talk about mushrooms," she said at last, and a few kids groaned.

The jar was a little misty inside, like the mushrooms had been breathing, fogging it up. I handed the jar to Heidi in the front row to be passed around. Some of the kids sent it right on down the line, without even looking at it. I realized the kids who did all lived in my part of town.

"Some of you have probably seen them already," I guessed.

"Duh. They're in my yard," said the other kid named Eric in my class. "I'm already sick of them."

"My dog ate one and threw up," said Monica.

"Well, I, uh . . . I don't like them either, but I wanted to know more about them." I stammered through what I knew about the honey fungus—that it was all one great big fungus that was who knows how old, and that most of it lived underground. That it was like an underground tree with a trunk at the center and a lot of limbs coming out every which way. That the branches grew close to the surface, and the mushrooms popped up aboveground. Ms. Weller didn't correct me about anything, so it must have all been true.

"But why do they light up?" one kid asked.

"I don't know," I admitted. "The article wasn't very specific." A few kids laughed.

"They light up because they consume wood so quickly," Ms. Weller said. "They need to get rid of energy or they'll burn up, so they give that energy off as light."

"I've seen Eric eat," said Tom. "I'm surprised he doesn't light up." The class roared, and it was pretty funny, I have to admit.

"I heard they turn red," said Tony when the laughter died down, "and then they blow up."

"I think that only happens in video games," I told him. The class laughed again.

"Do they burn you when you touch them?" a kid named Michael asked.

"No," I said. "At least I don't think so." I wasn't sure because I hadn't touched any.

"Why don't you reach into the jar and find out?" Heidi suggested.

"Ah, those mushrooms are old and half dead," said Michael. "I mean the live ones."

"Well, let's go get some fresh ones, then," she said. "There's plenty on the football field."

"What?" Tom leaned forward at his desk. "I was there yesterday. It was fine."

"They must spread fast," Heidi said. "Now there are mushrooms all over it."

"But we have a game tomorrow!" said Randy.

"Not just any game," said Tom. "A championship."

"Nobody told the mushrooms," she said.

A few kids ran to the window, but we were on the wrong side of the school to see the field.

"Can we go look?" I asked the teacher. "It's scientific discovery."

"I suppose," she said.

So the class herded out of the school and to the football field, which, like Heidi said, was overgrown with mushrooms. It could have been worse. They were mostly in one corner, spreading out across the back of one end zone and down one sideline to about the thirty-yard line.

"They aren't even lit up now," said Michael.

"It's hard to see the glow in daylight," I told him.

Heidi dropped to her knees, cupped the mushrooms with her hands to create a dome of darkness, and peered into the gap between her thumbs.

"It's true! They're lit up!" She looked at her hands. "They're not warm." I reached down and brushed my fingertips along the caps. It was the first time I'd actually touched them, and they felt like normal mushrooms, cool and a little slippery. You'd never know they were gobbling up nutrients so fast they were burning up.

"Will you guys be able to play?" a girl named Mary asked Randy, who was just now catching up to the rest of us on his crutches. Mary was on the pep squad and was probably looking forward to the game as much as the players were.

"They'll take care of it," he said. "And if they don't, we'll play anyway."

Coach said the same thing later.

"There's some guys coming to look at the turf," Coach said, "so we'll have to keep this short. But it's our last practice before the big game, and we have to figure out a new plan for our offense."

We took the least mushroomy part of the field to practice some new offensive plays. The defense was only in there to scrimmage, a two-hand touch counting as a tackle. On about the eighth make-believe tackle for a loss of yardage made by me, Tom gave me a non-make-believe shove.

"What are you doing, Beauchesne?" Coach shouted at Tom.

"Blocking."

"The play was over a minute ago. If this were a real game, you'd get a fifteen-yard penalty. Do you think the offense can even net fifteen yards at this point?"

"Well, tell him to stop being a jerk." He pointed at me. "He won't let us do anything."

"He's not supposed to let you do anything. It's called

'defense,'" Coach hollered back. Some of the kids laughed, and Tom glowered.

We lined up again. I inched up from my middle linebacker position before the ball snapped, ready to blow past the guard and level the quarterback. Tom got antsy and snapped the ball too hard. The guy playing quarterback this series couldn't hold on to it, so I plunged past the line and scooped it up.

"Take it easy, man." I handed the ball to Tom.

"Thanks for nothing, jerk," he spat out. He got right in my face and whispered, "If you hadn't broken Randy's leg, we wouldn't have to worry about any of this."

Maybe Tom and Will weren't ratting on me, but they hadn't forgiven me either.

He gave me a big shove, and I shoved him back, which we're not supposed to do, but sometimes you shove first and think later, and this was one of those times.

He tried to shove me again, and I grabbed his arm.

He yanked it loose. "I'm not your little brother, Parrish. You can't pull that WWE junk on me."

We're both big guys and neither of us is easy to shove around, but we shoved each other all over the field. I finally got my shoulder into his chest and sent him backward onto a padding of mushrooms, which was lucky for him. Coach was blowing the whistle the whole time, but it was like a million miles away. I could practically feel steam blasting out of my ears at that point.

"Hit the showers, Parrish!" he shouted. "Chains, you go

sit on the bench until he's done." Coach knew better than to send us both in at once.

I left the field, stomping on as many mushrooms as I could on the way. I wanted to crush something to bits, and for now they'd have to do.

Chapter 10 THE UNDEAD SCHOOL

The shower cooled me off, and by the time I got dressed, I was sorry. Maybe this time the coach really wouldn't let me back. I didn't want to face anybody. The locker room was between the gym and the field. I went out through the gym side rather than walk by Coach and everyone again. I slung the equipment bag over one shoulder, my backpack on the other, and my helmet under my arm.

I struggled a bit with everything as I walked home. I should have left the helmet in the locker room, I decided as the backpack slid off my shoulder and down to my elbow for the eleventh time. Somebody would have put it away for me. I probably didn't even need it anymore.

"Psst. Pig Boy! Want some help?"

I wheeled around and saw Mandy.

"What are you doing here?"

"I was using the computers at the library. I saw the guys playing football and wanted to see if you were there."

"I was, but I left early. I thought you had the whole Internet on your phone."

"Not really. The library has access to all kinds of stuff

you can't get at from any computer. Newspaper archives. Special collections at other libraries."

"Ooh . . . how exciting." Ms. Weller would have loved her.

"I found some interesting stuff, so there. Getting to a real library was half the reason I split in the first place."

"You weren't worried about anyone seeing you?"

"I didn't talk to anyone. I just sneaked in and found a computer in the corner."

"I thought you needed a library card to log in."

"I have ways," she said.

I could see the players trotting off the field in the distance, Coach clapping his hands and yelling something. The groundskeeper was already at the far end of the field, giving the mushrooms a series of little blasts with his sprayer.

"Hey!" said Mandy.

"Huh!" I'd sort of zoned out.

"I'll buy a pizza if you get it," said Mandy. "I have plenty of money, but my face is stapled to telephone poles all over town."

"All right. I could go for a pizza." I struggled to get the backpack back on my shoulder—it had slid down to my elbow again.

"Give me that," said Mandy, taking the helmet.

We walked toward downtown. Mandy turned up her collar to hide her face when we hit Keatston Street, and stayed so close behind me that she kept bumping me with my helmet. I called Dad from Mandy's phone, but she made me use an app routed through something called a proxy so she wouldn't show up on our caller ID. Dad picked up.

"Hello?"

"It's me."

"How come the caller ID says you're in Fresno?"

"It's been acting up lately. I'm calling from the . . . from Tom's cell."

"Okay, 'cause I'd be really ticked if you went off to Cali without me. Hey, I went shopping! Got all kinds of stuff that isn't made out of mammal."

"Great, thanks."

"I know you don't eat pig, and I went veg in Boston. Of course it's easy there, because there's so many awesome restaurants."

"Well, I'm going for pizza with some of the guys tonight, Dad," I cut in. Mandy and I were nearly in town. It was only a few minutes' walk from the school.

"Okay, cool beans. Talk to you later, bud." He clicked off.

Mandy took the phone and called her mom's house, getting her little sister. They argued a bit before she hung up, but I guessed that she would tell her parents that Mandy was okay.

"Little sisters," she said. "They're almost as bad as *big* sisters. You're lucky you don't have one."

"No, just a brother." I didn't remember talking siblings with her, but I must have. "He can be a pain too, but mostly he's a cool little kid. You'd like him. He likes monsters."

"Then he'd love my little sister," she said.

I got a Papa's pizza for takeout, which Mandy and I took to the empty pavilion at the park. We ate the pizza fast, since it was already getting cold. We'd settled on hamburger, since I didn't want sausage and neither of us wanted mushrooms.

"Oh, let me show you what I learned at the library." She dug in her bag and pulled out a stack of paper, riffled through it, and handed me a page. It was too dark to make anything out, but she fiddled with her phone and turned it into a rectangle of brightness.

"Flashlight app," she said, handing me the phone. "Read quick. That really drains the battery."

It was an article from the *Portland Press Herald*, dated October 1932 and featuring an illustration of mushrooms and a few lines of explanation: glowing mushrooms were spreading like wildfire in northern Maine. The mushrooms in the drawings looked like the ones from the magazine except they weren't in color.

"Guess who drew the picture?" Mandy asked.

"Max Bailey?"

"Yeah. How did you know?"

"I read his bio. I knew he was an illustrator for the newspaper."

"Well, now you know the mushrooms in that picture were real. They were in Maine, and they looked exactly like ours. But I couldn't find one more word about them in the Portland paper archives. It was like they lost all interest. Somehow FDR getting elected president was more important."

"Maybe there was nothing more about them because there was nothing else to report?"

"Max Bailey quit his job just after this illustration appeared. Something must have happened to him."

"His wife died."

"That happened years before he quit his job. Something might have happened *here*. He quit his job and moved so he could work on a story he never even *published*. Like he couldn't even bring himself to write about it. It's all connected. He saw something or discovered something that changed his life."

"Like a mushroom monster?"

"Maybe."

"I don't really see the point of all this," I admitted. "Even if Max Bailey did see the exact same fungus and even if it did turn out to be a monster, how does that help us?"

"I'm gathering facts," she said. "Don't you watch tape of other teams, Mr. Football? Look at the opponents' statistics?"

"We don't do that in middle school," I said. She had a point, though.

"Well, that's what I'm doing," she said. "You can't have a strategy if you don't know what you're up against." She reached out for the phone. "You're wasting the battery."

"Oh, yeah." I gave it back and she put it to sleep. "Hey, can I ask you something else?"

"I guess."

"So maybe you left Alden to save us all from the mushroom monster. But why did you get sent to Alden in the first place?"

"First of all, I didn't leave Alden to 'save us all from the mushroom monster.' I left to investigate a peculiar phenomenon. Second, Alden is an exclusive boarding school. I got *accepted* at Alden because I'm an excellent student."

"Ha."

"Ha yourself. Academically, it's top-notch."

"Maybe it is, but everybody around here says it's for girls . . . well, girls who are in some kind of trouble." Mom never said so, but I'd heard guys at school making jokes about it. It wasn't a reform school, but I knew it was really strict for a reason.

"It depends on what you mean by 'trouble,'" she said. "Some of the girls were just dating boys their parents didn't like. Or they dyed their hair pink and got a nose ring. It's only trouble because their parents didn't like it."

"So your parents didn't like your boyfriend?" Her hair was normal and she didn't have any piercings, so I guessed that was it.

"I've never had one, so no."

"So what did you do?"

"What makes you so sure I did something?"

"Because you're there. And you ran away instead of just telling your parents you hate it there, which makes me think they won't let you go home."

"Fine. I'll tell you what I did. I wrote a story. Huge crime, right?"

"You mean, like, fiction? A made-up story?"

"A made-up story called 'The Undead School.'"

"What happened?"

"It was about how everybody at my school turned into a

zombie, right? It's not going to win horror novel of the year, but it was okay. I posted it on the Internet as a blog. I put up a new chapter every few days. Some people even said they liked it, but some girls totally freaked out, and there was a big drama at the school."

"Drama?" I wasn't following her at all. What was the big deal about writing a story about zombies? Stephen King did a book about zombies, and he was the most famous writer in the state. Dad had a lot of his books.

"It was completely stupid," she said. "They said it was threatening. Even though I made up the names. Like Esmé Myer became I. Mimi Mine. And Ashlee Grant became Ain't She Grand. I changed names to protect the not-so-innocent, and it's not *my* fault people knew who I was talking about."

"Oh." I was starting to get it.

"The hero is this girl named Mary Killer," she continued. "She knows kung fu and stuff. She takes out the zombies one by one."

"And Mary is based on you?"

"Sort of, yeah. I mean, it's not a memoir or anything. . . ."

"So you posted stories on the Internet about you killing other kids."

"They were zombies," she said with a sniff. "What was I supposed to do?"

"I don't know." I mulled it over for a while. I could see other kids freaking out. I could especially see their parents freaking out.

"Not you, too!" she said.

"I didn't say anything."

"You don't have to. I see the look on your face. It's the same way my dad looked when he found out I was expelled."

"They expelled you for that?"

"Yep. Because I quote-unquote *threatened* other students. Zero tolerance for that at my school." I saw a tear roll along her nose. She took one of the pizza napkins and dabbed at her face. "This is greasy," she said, looking at the dirty napkin.

I gave her one of my unused napkins, and she wiped the grease and tears off her face.

"Where am I going to sleep tonight?" she asked. "I'm practically homeless."

"You could go back to Alden and . . . man up?" I said, using Coach words and wishing I hadn't.

"You want me to turn myself in?"

"Yeah." It would also send my dad back to Boston, but I was beginning to think it would be best for Mandy not to be practically homeless. I wouldn't tell on her, now that we were friends, but that didn't mean I couldn't nudge her to turn herself in.

"I can't," she said. "I hate that place so much."

"It can't be that bad. It's not like they can . . . cane you, or whatever."

"No, but Mrs. Bearish will take my phone, and they'll stick me in the RC, and then I won't even have access to the outside world. That's torture for me. Disconnecting somebody from *everything*. I don't have any friends there, and it gets lonely."

I was going to ask what an RC was, but the question got shoved aside. "Mrs. Bearish?"

"This great big bear of a woman at the school."

"I think you mean Parrish. That's my mom."

"Really?" She looked at me. "Oh, yeah. Your name is on your uniform. E. Parrish."

"That's me."

"We call her that because she's like our Mama Bear, you know? Looking out for everyone?" She saw I wasn't buying it. "I'm sorry. Girls are snarky and awful."

"Forget it."

"Okay, I am too, obviously," she said. "I didn't mean anything when I wrote that story. It seemed funny while I was writing it. I didn't think it would actually scare anyone." She sighed. "So I guess I can't spend the night at your house?"

"Ha. You definitely don't want that. Mrs. Bearish will be there." I thought hard. "Maybe we can figure something else out."

"Oh, I'll be all right," she said. "There are some empty houses around. There's usually a key under the garden gnome."

"Wait, I got it." I snapped my fingers. "It wouldn't exactly be breaking and entering."

Chapter 11 THE DARK MAZE

"What are you supposed to be?" the guy at the front door of the haunted house asked me.

"Huh?"

"She's a football player. I figured you were in a costume too. It's half price if you are."

Mandy was wearing my uniform over her street clothes, the helmet hiding her face.

"Here." Mandy reached through the face mask on the helmet to take off her Harry Potter glasses and put them on me. Everything went blurry. "I'm a jock, and he's a nerd."

The guy gave us a thumbs-up and the discount.

Mandy took her glasses back as soon as we were in so both of us could actually see. We stopped to look at the three bears eating Goldilocks.

"Truly horrible," Mandy said with a shudder.

"They really want to scare people," I told her.

"Or at least gross us out," she said. I felt proud of Tanglewood for having a good enough haunted house to even gross out a big horror fan like Mandy. We went past the bears and the headless horseman.

"What's this?" Mandy asked when we got to the WELCOME TO KEATSTON sign.

"It was the town that was here before Tanglewood, back in colonial days. It disappeared in seventeen-something."

Another group of people came by. I nudged Mandy out of the way so they could see.

"Lame," one of them said as they passed. They were obviously from out of town and didn't know the story behind it.

"The whole town disappeared?" Mandy asked in a whisper.

"Yeah, and so will we." I slipped through the curtain, and Mandy followed.

"What the heck?" She was stunned to find another room hidden by the curtains. I knew the room was here because I'd sat in here and watched films or listened to some old guy talk about artifacts half a dozen times.

"This is the old Keatston Meetinghouse," I explained. "The big part is where they had meetings—that's what they called church—and this is where the preacher guy lived. It's the only building that survived."

"Were they Puritans?" Mandy asked.

"It was later than that, but they acted like Puritans," I told her, remembering one of my school visits. "There was like a Puritan revival."

"Oh, yeah," she said. "We learned about that in history."

The room was crammed full of all the museum cases that were usually on display: table-sized clear plastic boxes full of old stuff. We squeezed between two cases, me trying to suck in my gut so I could fit. We finally found a padded bench where we could sit down. We sat with our backs to the cases and our feet on the wall.

"I figured you could hang out here," I told her. "I didn't think about it being crammed full of stuff."

"It's that much easier to hide," she said. She swiveled around to look at the cases. "I'm going to live in a museum, just like Claudia Kincaid."

"Who?"

"Never mind. So what did you mean when you said everyone disappeared?"

I told her about the fire with no ashes, the people of Keatston vanishing off the face of the earth.

"This was the only building left standing, and they never found bodies or graves or anything. They did find people's belongings. That's what's in all those cases: dishes and clothes, some letters, stuff like that. It's sad to see it."

There was a battered gray leather ball, now flat and torn and shriveled up like a raisin. The tour guide would point it out: "Whoever made that ball must have kept it hidden, because the town fathers would not have approved of such games." I always wondered what kind of secret sports those kids played. There were other taboo items in the cases—a tiny chess set and a pack of playing cards, a paintbrush with its bristles long gone, and a disintegrating copy of *Gulliver's Travels*. I thought mostly about the ball, because I couldn't have lived without some kind of sports. I wouldn't have been able to be me.

"It's sad to see it," I repeated.

"Hm," she said. She grabbed her phone, maybe to see what the Internet knew about Keatston. I was sitting in an uncomfortable position, but the room was dark and peaceful. I closed my eyes and dozed off for a while.

I woke up cramped and sore. I wondered what time it was, and whether or not Mom or Dad had started calling all of my friends to find me.

Mandy was gone. I felt around and found my sports bag. She'd put my uniform and pads back into it and set the helmet right next to it. Had she made another escape? No, her backpack was sitting right next to my stuff.

I turned and tried to make out anything in the darkness. I saw a faint light bobbing near the doorway and felt my way there, scraping and gouging myself against several museum cases on the way.

"Mandy?"

"Yeah. Look at this." She had her phone turned back on flashlight mode, the light dimmer than it was earlier. The battery was probably on its last gasp.

"What time is it?" I asked her.

"It's only nine-thirty. They shut down half an hour ago. Look." She directed the faint flashlight beam at something on the wall.

It was the famous picture of Keatston, showing the town swallowed up by fire. It's kind of cartoonish but not comical. In fact, I bet the picture gave every kid who ever saw it nightmares: rings of red and blue flames radiate from the Meetinghouse, the colors faded over time but still visible.

Everything else is uncolored—the square rustic buildings consumed by the blaze, the tiny people with their arms waving and their mouths little O's of fright. The Meetinghouse itself is at the center of the inferno but untouched by fire. There's a window at the side and a boy looking out, his eyes wide. He isn't screaming but he looks scared. It's the same window we were just sitting under.

"Who drew it?" she asked.

"Nobody knows, and it's not exactly a drawing." I told her what I remembered from the tours—that the picture was a block print, meaning the artist did it backward in wood, cutting away everything but the lines to make a giant stamp. He'd coated the stamp with ink and pressed it on the paper, then colored in the fire with watercolors handmade from berries. Maybe he'd used the brush that was now lying in one of the cases.

"You know, those don't look like flames," she said. "They look like mushroom caps."

I looked again, and sure, they did look like the conical mushroom caps, but they also looked like soft-serve ice cream or gnome hats, depending on how you looked at them. It probably wasn't easy to carve super-realistic-looking fire.

"They keep coming back," she said in a whisper. A centipede with very cold feet ran along my spine.

"We need more evidence," I said, using her own words from earlier. "Let's gather facts." I searched the picture for some clues. Why couldn't the words say something useful, like "Ye Olde Toade Stooles," instead of that stuff about the seeds of redemption?

"They are mushrooms," she said. "I'm sure of it." Her light flickered and dimmed. "Uh-oh. I need an outlet so I can charge up my phone."

"And use the flashlight to find an outlet to charge it up?"

"Exactly," she said. "Oh, but I left the cord in my bag in the other room."

"Maybe we can find a light switch?" I stretched my hands out and took baby steps until I found the wall, then started groping around.

"No. Somebody might see the lights through the windows."

"Good point." I gave up my search.

"There's some jack-o'-lanterns by the headless horseman," she said. "I bet they have little lights in them."

"Oh, good thinking."

"Can you please go get one?" she asked.

"Me? Why me?"

"Because it was my idea."

"Fine." I found my way through the curtains to the haunted house, crashing into the make-believe welcome sign. I reached out in front of me until I found the canvas wall of the maze and went left. The pumpkins were that way, in the corner. I took a few small steps, scared that I might trip and bring down some of the walls.

I heard a noise behind me and pictured the witch in the maze with me, following me, ready to reach out and tousle my hair. That ice-footed centipede was back, and he'd brought a bunch of friends to line-dance.

Stop freaking yourself out, Parrish, I told myself. Get a grip.

I accidentally kicked something soft and heavy, probably

one of the pumpkins. I stooped down and found it rolled over sideways. I took off the top and felt around inside its pulpy orange skull until I grabbed a pumpkin light about the size of a quarter. I ran my finger along the surface and flicked a switch. My prize for all this was a little halo of light about a foot in diameter.

A moment later the building was filled with light. Somebody had flipped on the overheads.

"I heard something down that way," someone shouted. It sounded like Officer Withers. He came to the school sometimes, telling us to say no to drugs.

"Stop! Who's that?" another voice shouted. I peeked around the wall and saw another policeman down the corridor, waving his flashlight at the black curtain leading to the back room. He must have heard Mandy.

Even though I thought Mandy should go back to her school, I thought it should be her decision, and for some reason I felt stupidly heroic. I picked up the slightly damaged pumpkin, stepped out into the corridor, and hurled it with all my might.

The officers jumped back as the pumpkin smashed to the floor and spattered their shoes. Before they looked up again, I was headed down the maze the other way. I took a wrong turn and ended up in the room with the three bears. I threw myself behind the display, watching two sets of feet run past me. The taxidermy bears reeked of wet dog and old rug.

The wood-and-fabric wall behind me had a flap for a door, maybe so the haunted house actors could get around. I slipped through and found myself in the make-believe graveyard.

"You see anything up there?" Officer Withers hollered to the other cop.

"No, and the front door's barred shut. He must be hiding in here somewhere."

"Go secure the back entrance," said Officer Withers. "I'll flush him out."

"Make sure he doesn't have any more pumpkins," the other cop said.

If they caught me, I'd be in a lot of trouble because of that pumpkin. So it was best that they didn't catch me. I'd have to get out the back door before that other cop got there.

I jumped out into the corridor right in front of him.

"You!"

I froze. He would have grabbed me, but one of the maze walls came crashing down on top of him. He stumbled into the opposite wall, knocking that one down and flattening some tombstones.

The cop was sandwiched between the two rectangles of wood and fabric, and Mandy was sitting on that canvas-and-cop sandwich like a sprig of parsley.

"Go!" she shouted.

"No, you go! You're the one who's wanted."

Officer Withers appeared in the graveyard, having shoved some of the walls out of the way. He didn't have his gun out, but his right hand was hovering near the grip.

"Stop right there!" he hollered.

"You go!" I yelled again at Mandy, and tackled the policeman.

Chapter 12 STILL MISSING

"At least he didn't break anyone's leg," Dad told Mom on the drive home. "If we're looking for a bright side, there's that one." He smiled at her hopefully, but she was driving and kept her eyes on the road without even a glance in his direction. "It could be worse is all I'm saying," he said.

I'd remained silent all the way through the ordeal at the police station. I'd been told I had the right to, so I did. The cops had grilled me about what I was doing at the haunted house, what I was thinking when I threw that pumpkin, who my accomplices were, and a bunch of other stuff. I'd kept my mouth shut. Eventually they'd called Mom and Dad to come get me. They'd said they'd let me know when my court date was.

Now I was slouched down in the seat. I was exhausted. Remaining silent is hard work.

"Is Eric going to jail?" Brian asked. He was in the back with me, bouncing from excitement. I didn't think he actually wanted me to go to jail, but I could see things from his perspective—if I went to jail, he'd have something cool to talk about at school.

"No," said Dad. "If anything, he'd go to a juvenile detention center."

"That's like prison for kids," said Brian.

"It's not as bad," Dad said. "I saw a story about this joint near Boston where the kids live on a farm. They get to go horseback riding and everything. But they also have to do all the farm duties, so they can learn values. It didn't seem that bad. No different from the way kids lived for most of American history."

"Maybe Eric can go live on a pig farm," Brian suggested. "He'd like that."

Mom hit the brakes for a red light. We all lurched forward, then backward. "Your son is not a delinquent," she said. "And he is not going to a juvenile detention center."

If she'd known who my accomplice was, she might have changed her mind.

We turned down our street. The car made soft little bumps as it rolled over stripes of mushrooms that had broken across the road. There were mushrooms sprawled out across all the lawns, wrapping around trees, and climbing up the sides of houses.

"You've got lots of 'splainin' to do," Dad said when I went down for breakfast. I think he was impersonating somebody, trying to make it easier on me by being funny, but my brain was too addled to figure out who he was supposed to be.

"Lots of explaining," Mom agreed.

"I have the right to remain silent," I reminded them.

98

Mom had told me that herself. I opened the fridge so I could hide my head in it for a few seconds.

"Maybe with the cops," I heard Mom say. "Not with your parents."

The refrigerator was filled with fruit. I knew Dad had gone veg, but it also looked like he'd gone fruity. I took an apple and crunched into it, keeping my mouth full so I didn't have to say anything while Mom recapped the charges against me: breaking and entering, assaulting a police officer, vandalism.

"You've gotten yourself into some pretty thick soup in a short amount of time," she said.

I shrugged. What else could I do? My mouth was full of apple.

"You're grounded until further notice," she said. "Do you still have to take care of your pig?"

I nodded. It was Thursday. Michelle wouldn't be back until the weekend.

"Then you can do that," she said, "but no football."

I swallowed. "The championship game is today, and they need me for that."

"You should have thought about that before you got into the soup," she said.

"Aw, let the boy play football," Dad said.

"What?" She shot him a look that would have taken the pink off a pig, but Dad barely noticed.

"You can't take football away from him. That's his dream. . . ."

"You and your dreams!" Mom slammed her coffee cup

down, causing a minor caramel-colored tsunami to come crashing over the rim and splash onto the table.

He looked at me and shook his head—not his whole head, just his eyes, so Mom couldn't see him doing it. Shifting them back and forth, from side to side, then shifting them up and down, nodding—telling me that everything was fine, I would get to play in the championship game that day. Mom would be at work and wouldn't know until it was too late to do anything about it. There was no way she'd come home before the game was over, especially if Mandy was still missing.

But was she? I didn't know what had happened to her after I got arrested. Maybe she'd been caught after she left the museum.

"Hey, did they find that girl?" I asked, trying to sound natural.

"Don't change the subject," said Mom. "We're talking about you."

"I was just hoping she was okay."

"She's still missing," Dad whispered, getting another angry look from Mom.

I did want to do something minor to make things better, so I got a paper towel and blotted up the coffee. When I opened the cabinet under the sink to throw it away—that and my apple core—I saw a few tiny mushrooms breaking through the woodwork, scattered along the cabinet floor, a few more scaling the walls. I threw my garbage in the can and shut the door in a hurry.

When I went back up to my room to get my stuff, the

carving Brian had found was sitting on my desk, a sticky note next to him. "This is for luck," it said. The note didn't say if he was giving the carving to me or if he was just lending it to me, but I was touched either way. I looked into the colonist's tough wooden face. "Bring me luck, buddy," I told him, and stuck him in my hip pocket.

I stopped and took care of Cassie, then plodded through the school day. It didn't seem like anyone knew about my run-in with the law, but it was hard to say. They were all talking about the mushrooms, which now blanketed the school grounds, edging up the outside wall and in a few cases poking through the corners into classrooms. I wondered if the probing cords would gradually crumble the foundation and bring down the walls. Just like they did to Keatston, if that's what happened to Keatston.

I realized halfway through my second class that I didn't have my football uniform. It was either still at the museum or in the evidence room at the police station. The game was right after school, so I took off during lunch period and ran downtown. I was seriously sucking wind by the time I saw the haunted house and realized it was closed. Of course it was. There was no point in having it open when all the kids were in school and all the grown-ups were at work. I stopped to catch my breath. There was a pounding sound coming from inside—somebody hammering the heck out of something. I went around back and saw a handyman's van parked in the alley.

I found a side door propped open with a brick, sneaked

in, and tiptoed past two men putting up a wall of the maze. They were repairing the damage Mandy and I had done. I slipped through the curtains and glanced at the ancient print of Keatston. Mandy's theory had gotten to me, and I now saw the licks of flame as mushroom caps. "The devil's fire may burn again," it said. It gave me a shudder. "God's wrath will purify the earth. The seeds of redemption are in the people."

I squeezed between the museum cases, glad for the sunlight streaming through the windows. My uniform was still beneath the bench, my helmet right next to it. The police must not have searched the place top to bottom. Maybe the museum people didn't want them crashing around among their artifacts.

When I passed the print the second time, my eyes connected with those of the boy in the window of the Meetinghouse. There was something familiar about him, like I knew him from somewhere other than this picture. It was a hard feeling to shake.

I crept past the carpenters and out of the building without being seen but got back five minutes late for science class. The room was dark, and nobody said anything when I slipped in and sat down. They were watching a documentary about snakes. A black mamba was making short work of a frog. Brian would have loved it.

Usually I get a surge of adrenaline before a game, but now that I really needed one, it didn't come. I crammed my clothes into the locker. My football pants didn't have pockets, so I had to tuck the carving into the belt, cinching him in so he wouldn't fall out.

Whatever the groundskeeper had done to the mushrooms hadn't worked. They were thicker and fuller than yesterday and blanketed the field. When we trotted out to warm up, there were already enough kids in the bleachers to do an Owls cheer—"Who's going to win? Whooo? Whooo?"—but the cheering fell silent when a few Owls players tripped and fell. I managed to stay up but did have a hard time finding my balance. The problem was obvious—our cleats were getting stuck in the spongy mass of mushrooms that covered the field.

"We can't play on this," one of the players complained, and a few others grumbled in agreement. Down at the other end of the field, the Blue River Oxen were having a lot more fun than we were, bouncing up and down on the mushrooms and laughing. They'd arrived but hadn't changed yet. They looked like little kids in one of those inflatable castles, and that gave me an idea.

"Take off your cleats," I suggested, and sat down on the field to take off my own. I ran across the field and dropped the cleats by the bench, enjoying the springy feel of the caps. It really *was* like being a little kid in a fun castle.

I noticed Dad and Brian in the bleachers about three rows back. Dad had never seen me play before, because he'd lived in Boston since I'd started getting playing time. I didn't think Brian had ever seen me play either. I waved, and they waved back.

"Score a touchdown!" Brian shouted. He must not have

known I was a defensive lineman, or he didn't know that meant I wouldn't ever score a touchdown unless I recovered a fumble or something.

Allan was there too, sitting by himself. I wondered why he wasn't sitting with Brian. Maybe he didn't want to hang out with a lowly fourth grader in front of his classmates.

The other guys kicked off their cleats too, and we went into our warm-ups. The QB kept lobbing the ball a little high so the receivers would have to spring up to get it, then take exaggerated tumbles across the spongy mats nature had given them.

"I think I'm faster than usual," Jake said, sprinting across the mushrooms to midfield and back again. He was probably slower, but he was right that it *felt* faster, with our legs bouncing off the rubbery mushroom caps.

And that's how we played the game. The only players who wore shoes were the kickers. Jake took the opening kickoff to about the thirty-yard line (we couldn't see the numbers) and got bounced on his back by a defender. He dropped the ball and it was picked up by an Oxen player who fumbled it himself a few seconds later. Our guys finally fell on it and ran a swing pass on the first play from scrimmage. It ended up as a touchdown, defenders diving and missing all over the field as the halfback lumbered by. The whole first half was like that: wild plays and pratfalls, touchdowns and turnovers.

"This game is a joke," Tom said in the locker room during halftime. Maybe he was saying that because we were losing by thirteen points.

"We can get it back," I said. It was a high-scoring game.

I'd lost track of the exact score, but thirteen points was nothing.

"The game is a joke," he said again. "I don't even care if we win. It's a joke. It was a joke without Randy anyway, but it's now an even bigger joke." He kicked at a locker and stubbed his toe. He forgot he wasn't wearing shoes.

I knew what he meant. The game didn't have the usual intensity. I hadn't thought about it much because I was having fun. Maybe it was boring to watch, too. The stands had emptied out a bit. I saw that Dad was still there and waved to him, but Brian and Allan were gone.

Early in the second half I scooped up a loose ball and bounded toward the end zone while the Oxen tried to catch up to me. One of them did, a guard who was nearly as big as me. He hurled all his weight at me and hit me like a barrel. I fell into the end zone, scoring my first ever touchdown, but I stumbled and banged my forehead on the post part of the goalpost. It was padded and I was wearing a helmet, but my head bounced back and there was an audible thud.

Colors pulsed and spun around in blackness, and my entire body felt like a computer in shutdown mode, one window after another closing, the screen fading to black, and then silence and nothingness.

"Hey. Hey. Are you okay?" The Oxen guard was kneeling over me, waving his fingers at me. Then Coach was there. I smiled and held up my hand, meaning to make a touchdown signal, but I couldn't. You need both hands for that. You need to be standing up, too, and I wasn't. I laughed at that—and wondered why Coach wasn't laughing with me.

He turned to talk to someone, his voice really far away. I slowly got up and walked back toward the bench, wobbling and feeling sick to my stomach. Coach caught up with me and helped me off the field. I sat down on the bench and tried to take off my helmet, then realized it was already gone. I'd lost it somehow.

"Nice score," said Randy. "Feels great, doesn't it?"

"Sure thing," I said. "Hey, shouldn't you be out there?"

He showed me his crutches and the cast on his leg.

"Oh, yeah." I couldn't remember what had happened to him, though. I watched the game for a few seconds, but I didn't feel like it mattered, really. They were kids in socks bouncing around on a field of marshmallows. It made me smile.

Then Coach was bugging me again, telling me to get up. I realized that it was our defense out there, and that he must want me to play. First I had to find my helmet. I stood up so fast I felt like a bird taking flight, like my feet were letting go beneath me, which they were.

Chapter 13 THE FALLOW FIELD

I woke up at the hospital, inside a big whirring machine. I realized that I was crying, but I wasn't sure why. Dad was walking by. No, skating by. He wasn't bobbing up and down; he was sliding off to the left. I grabbed at his wrist to stop him. No, he'd been standing still the whole time. I was the one moving. They were bringing me out of the machine.

"Who won?" I asked him. He shook his head.

"Please find out," I said. "It's important." But Dad didn't seem to think it was urgent at all. He reached out and patted my shoulder.

"You hit yourself in the noggin," he said.

"No I didn't. I ran into a pole." Dad didn't even know what had happened.

"That's what I meant," he said.

"Find out who won," I said again.

He reached for his phone. "Who do I call?"

I tried to remember Tom's number and couldn't. I tried to concentrate—the first number was a 5, I was sure of that, but then what? Before I could think of it, the doctor came back in with pictures of my brain. He pulled up a chair next to me and asked me how much I remembered. I explained it as best I could, and he nodded.

"You have a concussion," he said. "Do you know what that is?"

"It's when you get the senses knocked out of you." I'd seen guys on TV with concussions, and the dazed look in their eyes—it was scary stuff.

"Exactly," he said. He explained that in my case I'd bruised my skull and my brain along with it. Hearing it put that way made me want to throw up.

"It could be worse," said the doctor. "The CAT scan looks clean. Your pupils look good. The fact that you remember what happened is *really* good. You're going to be all right, Eric." He tapped me on the shoulder like I'd made a good play, which I guess I had.

He talked to Dad for a long time, but I couldn't follow it very well.

I was in one of those hospital gowns with the rear window, so I got up and got dressed in my football uniform, which was in a pile on a chair. I didn't really want to get back into sweaty, stretchy pants, but my street clothes were probably still in the locker room. Something was missing, but I couldn't think of what it was. I looked around for it anyway, until I got dizzy and had to sit down. I squashed a pile of pads under me and couldn't find the energy to move them. The doctor went on and on talking to Dad, who kept nodding. The doctor finally handed him a bundle of information and turned back to me. "The only treatment for a concussion is plenty of rest," he said. "So no school tomorrow, and no football for a few weeks, okay?"

"Football is done anyway," I told him.

One of my teammates had dropped my clothes off at the house. I poked through them and still couldn't find whatever it was that was missing. There were a lot of messages waiting at home for me too: Coach, Randy, Will, and a bunch of other people wanted to know if I was okay. They also told me that the Oxen won. I didn't care anymore. The game was a joke, like Tom had said. How many real football games are played shoeless?

I couldn't even make it through all the messages. My head was throbbing and I still felt sick to my stomach.

I went up to bed.

Brian came out of his room in his pj's. They had the hedgehog heroes from his last favorite video game, before he discovered Gninjas.

"Are you all right?"

"Just a little banged up."

"What got banged up?"

"Just my head. Nothing important."

"Do you have my little man?"

"What?" It took me a second to remember the colonist. The carving I'd kept as a good-luck charm. Lot of good it did.

"I lost it," I told him. That was what I'd been looking for

at the hospital, even though I couldn't figure out what was missing. "It might be on the field. I'll look later."

"Okay. Good night. Sorry you got hurt."

"Night. And thanks."

I replayed the touchdown over and over in my dreams, galloping toward the goal line and wishing I could go back in time and make myself swerve.

I woke up in the middle of the night and remembered I hadn't eaten anything since the apple I'd had that morning—or yesterday morning, since it was now well into Friday. Maybe a little food would make me feel better. I walked downstairs.

There was plenty of blue-green light shining through the glass of the back door and spilling across the carpet into the hallway. Or at least that's what I thought it was. When I got closer, I could see a row of mushrooms along the edge of the hallway near the family room. I reached down and pulled one up, ripping it out of the wood, breaking the tough little roots. I cupped it in my other hand and proceeded to pull up the rest.

I started across the family room to toss them out the back door, and I realized the floor was all wrong—soft and spongy, like there was an extra layer of uneven padding under the carpet. This room was added to the house after it was built, so there was no basement beneath it. The mushrooms had bored straight up from the ground through the floorboards.

When Dad came down an hour or two later, I had part of the carpet rolled back and was scraping at the floor with a putty knife.

"What are you doing?"

"Scraping up mushrooms," I told him.

"You're supposed to be taking it easy," he said. He came over and took the knife from me. "Are you sure you're okay?"

"No. My head hurts and I can't sleep. I'm sick of these mushrooms."

"Your mother is finally taking a day off. Let her sleep in. Come on—I'll make omelets."

"That would be great." I'd forgotten I was hungry.

I followed him into the kitchen. Dad cracked some eggs into a bowl and whisked in milk. "Do you want anything inside them?" he asked.

"No mushrooms," I said. "No bacon bits."

He made mine with cheese and smothered it with salsa. It was great. I shoveled bites into my mouth, trying not to think about fungus or football or anything else. Dad started making his own omelet when Brian came in, still in his hedgehog pj's.

"Do I have to go to school?" he asked.

"Um . . . why wouldn't you? Want some eggs?" Dad dumped the omelet onto a plate and handed it to Brian.

"Can I have ketchup?" he asked.

"I don't care. Why don't you want to go to school?" he asked.

"Because nobody else in the family is going to work or school," said Brian. He opened the fridge and got the ketchup. "It's not fair."

"Good point. Okay, take the day off. We'll all have a three-day weekend."

"Yay!" Brian sat down and drowned his eggs in ketchup.

Dad started a third omelet. I finished my own before Dad sat down with his.

"I better go take care of Cassie," I said.

"Oh, no you don't. You're supposed to be resting. First you scrape up the floor, and now you're going to go take care of a pig? It would be better to go to school."

"Somebody has to feed her," I reminded him. "Michelle won't be back until tomorrow or Sunday."

"I can do it!" Brian offered. "I've seen Eric do it. It's not that hard."

"It isn't, huh?" I said. "What would you do?"

"Give her the bag of food from the restaurant and water from the hose and sweep up the mess under the trough and brush her if she needs it."

"She might not let you close to her."

"I can still feed her and give her fresh water."

"True." I noticed he didn't offer to shovel, but that didn't need to be done every day. I figured he couldn't mess up the basics.

"Can he?" I asked Dad. I was feeling a little bit woozy, now that I thought about it.

"Sure. Go feed Eric's pig."

"Okay!" Brian finished his eggs in a hurry and left a moment later. I went back to bed after breakfast and slept like a stone.

I was awoken by Mom and Dad having an argument. Their voices were just loud enough to boom up through the floor, but not loud enough for me to hear what they were arguing about. I decided to clear out. I didn't want to hear them shout at each other.

I tried not to hear anything as I left the house, but I heard a few words—Mom telling Dad that he wasn't in college anymore, and that he wasn't just out of college either. Dad telling Mom that he knew how old he was because all he had to do was look in a mirror to see he was old, but old didn't mean defeated. I shut the door before they realized I was leaving.

From down the street I heard the *whap whap whap* of Allan practicing basketball. He saw me and ran over, still dribbling. He had good control over the ball, and I was impressed. He was winded by the time he got to me.

"Hey (*pant*), Eric (*pant*), good (*pant*) game yesterday (*pant*)." He took a deep breath. "I heard you got a concussion. I hope you're okay."

"I guess so." My head hurt, now that he reminded me about it. "How come you're not in school?"

"My asthma is really bad these days." He took another huge breath to prove it. "The mushrooms make it worse."

"Then how come you're outside?"

"It's worse inside," he said. "There's mushrooms in there, too."

"They bother you that much?"

"Yeah. I'm allergic to all kinds of fungus, mold, and mildew."

"Hey, do you want to play HORSE?" I asked. I needed to kill some time while Mom and Dad worked out whatever they were working out.

"Sure!"

He turned me into a horse right away.

Brian came up the street, waving at us from our driveway. I waved back.

"Want to play?" I shouted. Mom and Dad probably weren't done fighting, and Brian didn't need to hear that.

"Sure!" He trotted on over. Allan scowled. Maybe he just wanted this to be a big-kid game.

"Are you just getting back from taking care of Cassie?" I asked Brian. It shouldn't have taken him that long.

"I went looking for my carving," he said. "I couldn't find it."

"I'll look later," I promised.

"You go first." Allan bounced the ball hard at Brian and nearly took his head off, but he grabbed the ball in time.

"Easy, man," I said.

"I said I was sorry," Brian muttered to Allan. He bounced the ball and took his shot, rolling the ball on the rim and missing. I didn't know what was going on and didn't ask. We played three rounds. I invoked a no-layup rule, using my football injury as an excuse, but Allan still won all three games. By that time he wasn't mad at Brian anymore and even wanted to play a fourth round, but we were both horsed out.

Mom and Dad were still arguing when Brian and I got home.

"How is that my fault?" Dad was yelling.

"I didn't say anything was your fault," Mom said. "I was just speculating."

"Yeah, you were speculating all right. You're famous for your speculations."

"It's all right," I whispered to Brian. "Just boring grown-up talk."

We sneaked past the kitchen and hurried up the stairs.

We had dinner early. Mom and Dad just focused on their plates, not talking to each other. I cleaned up my own plate while Brian nibbled at his food, looking glum. He was probably thinking, like I was, that if Mom and Dad kept arguing, it would end with Dad leaving again, and soon.

"So how's your head?" Dad asked me, finally breaking the silence.

"Good." I'd taken another nap. It was a big help.

"So I was wondering if you wanted to go camping," he said. "It'll be warm enough—it's been a weird fall."

"What, tonight?" I asked.

"Why not?"

"Can we go to Moosehead Lake?" Brian asked, his eyes full of hope.

"I was just thinking the backyard," said Dad. "Since it's so last-minute."

"How about the big field at Michelle's house?" Brian asked. "It's more like wilderness."

"Sure," said Dad. "If you don't think she'll mind."

"I don't think so," I said. "That sounds great." Dad was good at putting up a tent and making a campfire.

"Isn't Eric supposed to be taking it easy?" Mom said. "Not to mention grounded?"

"What's easier than camping?" Dad asked. "It'll be fun and spooky with the mushrooms everywhere. I haven't spent quality time with them since I got here."

"Yay!" Brian said.

Camping did sound like fun, but I didn't agree that the mushrooms would make it *more* fun.

It was already getting dark when Dad pitched the tent close to the woods, not far from the pen but as far as he could from the compost heap.

"Not exactly the woodland smell I'm used to," Dad said, but he was in a good mood. We hadn't pitched a tent together in over a year, but it all came back to us. Dad unrolled it. Brian and I spread it out and smoothed the wrinkles with our hands. Then Brian and I tugged on opposite corners, trying to keep it as taut as possible while Dad put in the pegs. Brian used to make faces and struggle, but he did fine this time. The kid was growing up.

Michelle's house was dark and quiet, and I didn't know if Mandy was hiding there tonight or not. If she was, I kind of hoped she would come out and join us. I didn't think Brian would tell on her. I didn't even think Dad would tell on her.

After the tent was up, Dad measured off about ten paces and slammed a shovel into a patch of mushrooms, then started to dig out the fire pit. He had to drive his heel into the back of the shovel to force the blade through the stringy roots.

"These things are a lot tougher than they look," he said.

"I know."

He lined the hole with stones we found around the field and in the woods. It was going to be a tiny fire—not much for warmth, but enough for ambience and marshmallow toasting. Only we didn't have any marshmallows, because Dad didn't have a chance to go shopping for the campout. He said most marshmallows weren't vegetarian anyway— they were made with gelatin, which was made from cow hooves. He'd prepped some apples at home, coring them and stuffing the middles with butter and brown sugar, then wrapping each in tin foil. We tossed them into the fire, waited a bit, then rolled them out to the edge of the pit. The foil cooled off fast, so we could pick them up, but inside the apples were warm and gooey. Dad called them camping apples, and they were one of my favorite things in the world.

I looked up at Michelle's house again, sure that I saw a flicker of light in the window, but I decided it was just the moon reflecting in the glass. I noticed Brian looking that way too. He must have been trying to figure out what I was looking at.

Dad started strumming on his acoustic guitar, strumming and humming, like he didn't have any particular song in mind. It was hypnotic listening to him and looking across the fallow field, the shadows of trees dividing the two vast seas of light—mushrooms below and stars up above. The mushrooms seemed especially bright, like they were happy to be alive.

"Can you play that song about the horseman?" I asked him.

"What?"

"'Through the woodland, through the valley.' That one."

"Oh, yeah. 'Donkey Hotay.'" He plucked a string and turned one of the pegs.

"It's not a donkey, it's a horse."

"No. 'Don Quixote.' That's his name." He spelled it out for me, explaining it was based on some old novel. Somehow I never knew the guy really did have a name. Why did the lyrics keep asking "Who can the brave young horseman be?" if the answer was right there in the title? Dad played the song, and Brian and I started humming along, and for a few minutes everything was all right with the world. When we stopped, the guitar and our voices echoed over the field.

Brian and I had gotten bigger since the last time we'd been camping, and the tent was a tight fit. Dad fell asleep right away, but Brian was more restless, whispering and mumbling in his sleep. Before I could get comfortable, I heard a noise outside. It sounded human. I slipped out of the sleeping bag, put on my shoes, and crawled out into the mushroom-lit night. When I reached back to zip up the tent, my hand hit Brian's head. He was right behind me.

"I want to help," he whispered.

"Thanks."

We crept along the tree line so we wouldn't give ourselves away. There was definitely somebody at the sty. We heard voices, but no words—just a high-pitched chattering sound. It sounded like some little kids were mocking Cassie.

A moment later I saw what was going on and laughed. Against the backdrop of blue-green mushroom light were the silhouettes of two raccoons, one foraging in Cassie's trough, the other one perched on the roof of the shed, lifting its voice to chatter an emphatic warning. Cassie herself was inside the shed, probably sleeping and oblivious to this theft of her scraps. There were usually raccoons all over the place around here, but I hadn't seen any trace of wildlife since the mushrooms took over.

I'd never been happier to see an oversized rat. If raccoons were holding out, maybe there was hope.

The raccoon in the trough climbed out, turning its head to look at us with contempt. It wasn't afraid of us. It took its time waddling away, too, although from the size of its bottom, I'm not sure it could have run if it had to. It disappeared into the trees, and its little watchdog scampered after it.

"I like living here," Brian said in a whisper.

"Me too," I said.

Dad was up first and got the fire going again. I unwrapped the last apple and fed it to Cassie, who responded with a surprised grunt when she found the sweet buttery mess in the middle. Mom brought us a box of donuts and thermoses full of coffee and cocoa. I filled my tin cup with half of each and grabbed two donuts. That was my idea of a good breakfast.

We lingered until late in the morning. Mom hunched by the fire, holding her coffee. Dad strummed his guitar, and Brian played Cassie's favorite game, Feed the Pig Another Donut, until the box was empty. I poked at the fire and thought about everything. It was all going to fall apart pretty soon. Dad would move back to Boston. Brian would go back to being bratty. I might go to reform school. On top of all that, the mushrooms would continue to spread through town. The cords were sprawling out beneath us, making their way into the foundations and walls of our houses. The fungus could make the ground give way, the walls crumble—even if it didn't rise up from the earth and devour us all.

When Dad started pulling tent pegs to roll up the tent and go home, Brian cried.

Chapter 14 ROTTING FROM THE INSIDE

Dad and Brian went on a bug hunt. Dad thought it sounded like a blast.

"I can go too," I offered.

"You're supposed to be taking it easy," Dad said, which was fine with me. I relaxed in the living room and found a college game on TV. Mom settled down in the armchair with a historical novel.

"You're not working today?" I asked.

"It's Saturday," she said, as if that answered the question.

A moment later she got a call and went into the kitchen. I heard "She's not supposed to have a phone," and that was about it. I guessed it was more about Mandy. She wasn't supposed to have a phone at school, and now they'd figured out that she did. Next time I saw her, I'd give her a warning. In fact, I should probably try to do that right now.

I put my shoes on and headed for the door.

"I'm going to feed Cassie!" I shouted, since I was supposed to be grounded. Mom waved at me from the kitchen, the phone wedged between her shoulder and her ear. She didn't remember I'd just been there.

121

I didn't know where to look. Maybe Mandy was at Michelle's? The house had been as quiet as a graveyard last night, but it wasn't like she'd crank up loud music and turn on all the lights.

Michelle's jeep was parked in the driveway. I guessed that Mandy wasn't there.

"Eric!" Michelle hollered out of one of the kitchen windows. "Come on in—we need to talk." She waved me toward the back door. I wished she hadn't seen me. I was pretty sure what she wanted to talk about.

She'd made iced tea, and she poured me a glass as soon as I came in.

"How were the bears?" I grabbed a chair at the kitchen table.

"I didn't see any to ask," she said. "Usually they're at the birches around this time, but it's been so warm, the bears might be confused."

"Sorry."

"So what happened while I was gone?"

"Huh?"

"It looks like somebody's been living here. The refrigerator's been raided, and there was a pile of blankets on the couch."

"Oh." What could I say? That I was hungry? That I felt sick and took a nap?

Michelle must have seen the wheels turning in my mind.

"It wasn't you. There are long black hairs in the shower." She ran her hands through her own hair, which was short and gray.

"What happened, Eric?"

I took a swallow of tea to stall for time. It tasted fruity, like peach or mango or something. I didn't like it.

"Eric?"

"This girl broke in," I said. "I told her to leave but I think she came back." She might have run off through the woods when Michelle's jeep pulled into the driveway. No time to clean up or put things the way she found them. "She ran away from Alden. She's nice. She helped me take care of Cassie and I felt bad for her. I'm really sorry."

"Did you think about calling the police?"

"I thought about it. . . ."

"I don't know what to do," she said. "I mean, you really did take the best care of Cassie that you could have, but this is my home, Eric. I can't tell you how it feels to have a stranger living in my home. And what's worse is you didn't think about *her*. Who knows what will happen to her?"

"I'm really sorry," I said again.

"I'll take over all the pig duties for now," she said. "I'm not really mad at you, Eric, but maybe you're too young for this much responsibility."

"You mean I'm fired?"

"Let's call it an indefinite leave of absence," she said.

I left without finishing my tea.

Maybe Michelle had gotten back in the nick of time, if they were about to nab Mandy by tracking down her phone. Where would Mandy go next? I should have gotten her phone number. Of course if I had it, I'd call to tell her not to use her phone, and that would make no sense.

The only thing I could think of was the library, but she wasn't there. I checked the computer area, then walked through the stacks. It's a small library, and it didn't take long. There was no trace of Mandy.

I left the library feeling a little knot of dread in my stomach. I didn't especially want to go home. Even though Mom and Dad had made up, there was a bad vibe in the house. Not to mention fungus crawling up through the floorboards.

I glanced at the football field and remembered Brian's carving. He'd said he'd looked for it, but I could look too.

The mushrooms there had gotten tall on the field and tickled my ankles. I had to separate the caps with my hands and peer down between the stems. I started at the goalpost I'd smashed into and worked from there in widening circles until I gave up on the end zone and tried to retrace my path after the fumble. I finally found the carving in a clump of mushrooms under the bench where I'd sat for a few seconds before they'd taken me to the hospital.

It was broken. Not in half, but the head was tilted sideways. Some dust spilled out of the neck, like maybe it was rotting from the inside out. I tried to gently straighten the head, but it was permanently skewed. I'd thought of the little guy as grim before, but with his head cocked he looked a little sly.

I took the long way home. I didn't want to walk through woods full of mushrooms and was in no hurry to get back. On the way I heard the *chop-chop-chop* of a helicopter and looked up, wondering if it was a police helicopter searching for Mandy. It had a big 5 on it, the news station out of Bangor. Tanglewood was going to be on the news for something. The copter whirled out of town and into the woods. Of course— the fungus was going to be on the news.

Brian was playing Gninjas.

"Turn that off. I want to watch the news."

"I was here first."

"Come on, Bri. Tanglewood is going to be on!"

"Oh, all right." He turned it off and started out of the room.

"Don't you want to watch?"

"Nah."

"Wait, I have something for you. . . ." I found the broken carving in my pocket and handed it to him. "Sorry, it's a little messed up. I lost it during the game."

He looked at it sadly and tried to straighten the head but couldn't.

"I'm really sorry," I said again.

"It's okay," he said. "Things break." He went slowly up the stairs, still playing with the head and tapping out dust onto the steps.

I turned the TV to channel 5 but had to sit through some other stuff about an upcoming referendum, layoffs in Portland, and a house fire in Presque Isle before they showed our own neighborhood getting smothered by fungus. You couldn't see individual caps. It was a giant spongy mass taking up an acre of woods and spilling into town.

"Next: A small town in Hamlin County has a

mushrooming problem . . . with mushrooms," the news guy said. They went to a commercial break.

I had to sit through four or five ads before they came back, again showing the aerial footage of Tanglewood.

"What you see here is a *whole* lot of mushrooms," the anchorman said, dragging out the word "whole," sounding like a game show host. At that point Dad came in and said something about dinner.

"I'm watching the news." I pointed at the TV.

"And it's not even the sports segment," he said in surprise.

The news now showed a reporter talking to a neighbor from down the street, Mr. McNeil. "They're a serious problem," he said. He had a furrow in his brow the size of a canyon. "We can't get rid of them, and now they're in our house." There were snippets of interviews with half a dozen other people, all of them complaining about the mushrooms.

The phone rang, and Dad answered it. He hollered for Mom to come and get it. Why did everyone in the house have to make a racket the one time I was watching the news?

Dad joined me after handing the phone to Mom.

"Hey, that's Tanglewood!"

"Yeah, that's why I'm watching." I moved over on the couch so he could join me.

The last guy they showed was the grumpy guy who owned the hardware store. "I think we ought to spray 'em with every kind of pesticide and herbicide we got until they go away," he said, waving his hand to show that he had plenty of both on the shelf behind him.

"Wouldn't that kill the trees?" the reporter asked.

"Well, you can't make an omelet without breaking eggs," he said.

They switched back to the news anchor. "Some tempers flaring up in Hamlin County, but we are told the mushrooms will all go away after the first frost. Well, they might be disappointed by the weather report, which is next. But stay tuned, because we still haven't told you the most amazing part of this story, and it'll be easier to show you than tell you."

We sat through the weather and sports and a story about this lady's 104th birthday party and another batch of commercials to see the mushrooms at night.

"As promised, here's another look at those mushrooms in Hamlin County," the anchor finally said. "Sorry for the suspense, but we needed to wait for sunset."

It was pretty amazing, I have to admit. The fungus looked like a squid in an inky black sea. There was a black circle in the middle of the squid like a Cyclops eye. I knew it had to be the clearing where Brian and I had seen the mushrooms for the first time. The area was black now because the core had sucked all the nutrients out of the wood and the soil. Maybe that eye would get wider and wider as the fungus fed, eventually leaving nothing but a scar where Tanglewood and the surrounding woods used to be.

It did look kind of like a monster, but it wasn't really a monster, not the way Max Bailey drew it. It was worse: stupid and relentless and sneaky, slithering around beneath us where we couldn't even get at it without ripping the town apart. It would be better if it did rise up and fight—fight like a real monster.

Mom was still on the phone when we sat down to eat our tuna casserole.

"I thought you went veg," I said to Dad.

"I eat a little fish," he said. "Anyway, you kids need your protein."

We ate without talking much. We were halfway through dinner by the time Mom came into the kitchen.

"Well, we found Amanda," she said. "She's fine."

I dropped my fork with a clank. It was probably best Mandy wasn't practically homeless anymore, but I wondered how much they knew.

"Oh, that's great news," said Dad. "That's awesome."

"Yeah, that's great," I said. I retrieved my fork. "How did they figure out where she was? Did they find clues and track her down, or did somebody just turn her in? Did she have accomplices?"

"What's your sudden interest in all this?" she asked.

"I was curious how they find people. It's like a cop show, only real."

"Well, I don't know all the details," she said. "The important thing is that she's fine. I have to go in." She looked at the cold tuna casserole. "I'll grab something on the road."

"That's a huge relief," said Dad. "Huge."

Brian jumped up from the table and ran up to his room,

shutting the door with a little *thwunk* we could hear in the kitchen.

"What's wrong with him?" Dad said.

"I don't know," I said, which wasn't true. Dad had said he was staying until the Mandy crisis blew over. Now he was going to go back to Boston.

I finished Ms. Bearish's casserole and hoped she wasn't being too mean to Mandy.

An hour later there were cars cruising up and down our street, some pulling off and getting out of their cars to take pictures. We had folks trampling through our yards to get to the woods. I could hear Sparky from next door barking at the strangers as they trod across his territory.

"We're a tourist attraction all of a sudden," Dad said, watching people cross the lawn.

"More like a freak show," I said.

Chapter 15 AN EERIE AUTUMN

I slept until nearly noon on Sunday. Dad was sitting in the family room, paging through the book of Max Bailey stories. I must have left it on the coffee table.

"Are you reading these stories?" he asked.

"Um, yeah." I actually hadn't read any yet, I realized. "I'm going to, anyway. A friend at school recommended them."

"Good stuff," he said. "Hey, want some waffles?"

"Sure!"

Brian came bounding down the stairs.

"Can I play Gninjas?" he asked.

"Just be quiet," said Dad. "Your mom got home really late. Do you want some waffles? Because I'm making waffles."

"I ate *hours* ago," said Brian.

As we ate, Dad flipped through the newspaper and found the TV schedule. He told me the Pats were playing the Tennessee Titans at four o'clock.

"Oh, yeah."

"Aren't you usually all over this stuff?" he asked.

"Yeah, I guess so," I said. I had a lot more on my mind these days.

"I make a pretty good veggie chili," he said. "I can get it going in time for kickoff. We can watch one of the early games, too. I thought we could make a day of it. Football and food. A day for the guys."

"Sounds good."

I rummaged through the paper myself, looking for the sports section. I found the front section first, with a color picture of the woods at night riddled with blue-green mushrooms similar to the image from the TV news the night before. AN EERIE AUTUMN, the headline said. The story was about the woods, not the town—the dying trees and missing animals. I forgot all about the sports section and read the whole story. It was hard to get excited about the game when there was a fungus preparing to suck all the life out of the woods and maybe the town. It made me feel sick to my stomach, and it made me even sicker that people might go do more damage just to take care of it. They didn't have the guy from the hardware store in the article, but they had other people saying the same thing. Burn down the woods, spray them with poison, or rip up the ground. What was wrong with people?

I took the newspaper out to the family room, still hating the squishy mushrooms under the carpet.

As luck would have it, Brian was in one of the parts of the video game where mushrooms turned into monsters, one after another—swelling up and storming about until Brian's Gninja hacked them to pieces.

I should be doing something about the fungus, but what? Nobody knew. The article explained that. The reporter had interviewed some guy named Kowalski from the forestry department at the university in Orono. He talked about how frustrating it was. They couldn't roll in heavy machinery, ripping up the trees and churning up the ground, because they were trying to *save* the woods. He said that antifungal sprays were dangerous for the plants and animals and ineffective on *Armillaria mellea*, which was the scientific name for the honey fungus. The forestry professor took the same line as everyone else: we just had to wait for the first frost.

Brian eradicated the monsters, paused the game, and went to the menu. A moment later he was back in action. He was replaying the mushroom level over and over. It probably felt good. It was satisfying just to watch.

The last paragraph of the article sent my old pal the icy centipede skittering down my spine.

> This is not the first widespread outbreak of
> *Armillaria mellea* in Hamlin County, though few
> residents will remember the last one. That
> occurred in 1932, when the fungus devastated
> a hundred acres of forest west of Tanglewood
> close to the current infection site. Kowalski
> suggests it may even be the same fungus, as
> *Armillaria* is a hardy species that can live for
> hundreds—even thousands—of years. "The frost
> typically ends the fruiting, but it doesn't destroy
> the fungus," he said. "This thing may have been
> around longer than any of us."

I remembered what Mandy had said at the museum: "They keep coming back." The mushrooms do, that is. The fungus has been here all along.

Brian turned off the game. "I'm going to Allan's!" he announced, and left through the back door. The video game was off, and the TV was hissing static. The one o'clock game had started, but I didn't care.

I wanted to talk to Mandy. She'd been putting the pieces together and might know what to do. I didn't believe in the mushroom monster—but then, a few weeks ago, I wouldn't have believed a fungus could live for thousands of years.

Besides wanting to talk to her, I felt bad for Mandy. It wasn't my fault she ran away, and it wasn't my fault she got caught, but I felt partly responsible for her.

I popped into the kitchen, where Dad was stirring furiously at a pot, a few open cans of diced tomatoes on the counter.

"Browning the onions," he said. "It's going to be so good!"

"Do we have any Fritos?" I asked.

"Nope. Sorry."

"I like Fritos with my chili."

"You know what? So do I." He leaned the wooden spoon against the side of the pot, reached for his wallet, and handed me a five. "Do you think you can get back before kickoff?"

"Sure thing."

"Cool. Very cool." He grabbed for the garlic press.

I got my bike and pedaled madly down the street, making my way to the highway. At first there were mushrooms thick on my side of the highway, up the shoulder, with little jagged rows edging into the cracks in the asphalt. I plowed right through them. They petered out and disappeared at the Tanglewood city line, and after that it was smooth sailing.

I had a brisk tailwind, and it was an easy ride except for a few hills. There was a lot of traffic for a Sunday, and all of it going one way—probably more people headed up to see the amazing, spectacular, giant, run-amok fungus. They were missing out if they saw the mushrooms only during the daytime.

There was a long, gradual incline that wore me out a bit. I stopped at the top to catch my breath. Dad was probably wondering when I'd be back with the Fritos. How long would I be gone before he got really worried? How long before I got into trouble?

Well, I was going to be in trouble. There was no way around that, at least if Mom woke up before I got back. I would think of something. Excuses weren't hard to come by. I could get a flat tire or something. The chain could break on my bike. I could find a loose dog and take him home.

I looked back down the hill and saw two tiny bicyclers in the distance, making their way up the hill, standing on the pedals with every pump to put their weight into it. One wobbled and fell. It was Brian.

I spun my own bike around and rode back down the hill, already dreading the fact that I'd just have to ride up again. I braked hard when I reached the bottom. Brian was up but walking a slow circle to shake off the sting of the fall. Allan was straddling his bike, trying to catch his breath.

"What are you two doing?" I demanded.

"Nothing," said Brian. "Riding our bikes."

"You're following me."

"No, we're not!"

"Well, turn around and go home. I don't want company."

I rode back up the hill, stopping again to catch my breath. The second time was even harder than the first. I looked down the hill and saw Brian and Allan still standing at the bottom. I waved my arm toward Tanglewood and yelled.

"Go home!"

My words were carried away by the wind, but Brian and Allan started pedaling slowly toward home.

I moved on, going right past the sign for Alden Academy. A little bit farther I found a trail into the woods and stopped, made sure the coast was clear, and plunged in. It was a rocky trail, but I have a mountain bike with a tough frame, thick wheels, and a fixed gear so the chain wouldn't get knocked loose. I tried to keep my bearings as I twisted and turned on the path. I caught sight of a stately building, went off the trail, and locked my bike to a tree.

Mom had been working at Alden for years, but I'd never actually seen it. It looked more like a big house than a school and was surrounded by an eleven-foot-high fence. I hadn't thought about a fence.

I didn't think I'd find a garden gnome with a key in it, but I looked anyway. I walked around the school, keeping hidden in the trees. There was a back gate locked tight with a chain and padlocks. The front had an automatic gate and a gatehouse that looked empty. During the week there was probably a guard, but I guessed that on weekends the staff swiped a card at the box by the gate.

I was trying to figure out a way to get in when Brian came pedaling slowly up the driveway and stowed his bike in the trees on the other side. He didn't see me and I didn't want to shout. I picked up a pinecone and lobbed it at him, missing by a good ten feet. I'm not a quarterback. It was enough to get his attention. I sprinted across the driveway.

"I told you to go home," I whispered.

"You can't tell me what to do," he whispered back.

"Yes I can. I'm your big brother."

"No you can't!"

I knew from experience we could go back and forth like that for an hour. I didn't have the heart to fight with him, anyway. He'd skinned his palms and ripped his jeans when he fell off his bike, and he looked pathetic.

"Where's Allan?"

"He went home. I told him he could. His asthma was bothering him."

"You didn't go with him?" I remembered Allan's wheezing. "What if he needs help?"

"He told me it was okay. He said it happens all the time."

"You shouldn't leave a buddy all alone like that. Let's go catch up with him."

As soon as I said it, Allan appeared around a bend of trees on the driveway. Brian ran up and waved him off to the side.

"I. Decided. To. Come. Help," he said. He took an

inhaler from his pocket and inhaled deeply with it. "I'm fine," he said.

"Come help with what?" I asked them.

"Same as you," said Brian. "We're going to rescue Mandy."

"Mandy?" Why would Brian care about her? Because of Dad, I thought.

"Look, I'm not going to rescue her," I said. I hadn't thought that far ahead. I was just going to see what the situation was—how bad the school was, really, and how Mandy was doing. "I'm just going to talk to her. She can't stay a runaway forever, Brian. And sooner or later Dad's going to go back too. You can't make him stay here if he doesn't want to be here."

"I don't care," said Brian. "That's not why I'm doing it. I like Mandy."

"You don't even know her."

"Says you!" His eyes got fierce.

Maybe he did know her. Brian had taken care of Cassie on Friday. He must have met Mandy then. She might have been feeding Cassie when he got there. How else would he know that she was called Mandy? Mom always called her Amanda. Now that I thought about it, how else would he know I knew her?

Still, he'd only met her once, and based on that he was ready to set out to rescue her from the dungeon like a knight in a fairy tale?

"How are you going to help her, Bri?" I asked.

He reached into his jeans pocket and pulled out a keychain. I recognized the little hippo that Mom had for a fob. They were her work keys.

"At least I planned ahead," he said.

"Dude," I said, stepping forward to pick him up, then stopping because I remembered he didn't like that. "I was just looking for a garden gnome, but you're a freaking *Gninja*."

Chapter 16 THE SOUND OUTSIDE THE WINDOW

We still didn't have a way past the gate, but Allan threw himself on his Gninja sword. Nobody at the school would recognize him, so he found a pebble and used it to depress the valve on his bike tire and deflate it, rubbed some dirt on his face to look more pathetic, and went to the box on the gatehouse while Brian and I hid in the trees.

There was a big red button on it. Allan pushed it. There was no answer at first, but he held it down until a voice squawked at him.

"Can I help you?"

"I need help!" he said. "Can I use your phone and a bathroom?"

The squawking voice muttered something and went away. Several minutes later a woman came out and walked slowly across the lot.

"I got a flat tire and I'm really far from home and I was supposed to be home an hour ago but I can't walk that far and I don't have a bike pump. . . ." He rambled on a bit. The woman gave Allan the once-over and decided he wasn't a threat.

"We don't normally allow boys on the property," she

said. She keyed the box and opened the gate enough to let him in. He dropped his bike as soon as he was inside.

"There is a commode around back that the grounds staff uses," the woman said. "You can use that one. And you can use this for a phone." She held up a cell. "Which one do you want to use first?"

"The bathroom!" Allan said, now hopping from foot to foot.

"Well, good for you for not using the woods like some kind of animal," the woman said. She slid the gate closed and walked with him around the school.

"She didn't close it all the way," said Brian.

He was right. We slipped in and closed it behind us, jumped over Allan's bike, and sprinted across the parking lot to the other side of the school. If she'd locked the gate behind her, Allan would have faked an asthma attack just after she opened it to let him out. I was glad it hadn't come to that.

We found a side door and tried all the keys until one worked. The second we went in, we saw a flashing box.

"It's an alarm," I said.

"We have to hide," said Brian.

The alarm started screeching a moment later. We went up two flights of stairs, through some rooms and hallways, down another flight of stairs, around a corner, and down another hallway. We stopped when we heard footsteps and voices on the floor below, but they faded and we continued exploring.

The school looked more like Hogwarts than Tanglewood Middle School. There was fancy trim along the ceilings and floors, paintings hanging in the hallways carpeted stairs, and wooden railings. But Hogwarts would be fun, and this felt like the kind of place where you'd never be allowed to raise your voice and weren't supposed to touch anything.

"There's the offices," whispered Brian, waving at a sign. "Let's find Mom's."

We scanned the names on the doors until we found hers. Brian got the right key on the first try. We let ourselves in and shut the door behind us seconds before two women ran into the hallway.

"The offices are all locked," we heard one of them say. "Nobody's in there."

"Go do a head count in the dormitory," the other one said. "Brenda can search the school."

One woman left, and the other made a call. It sounded like she was pacing around in the hall right outside while she talked.

"See if you can find a map," I whispered to Brian, gesturing at the shelves. I started rummaging through the desk, and Brian sifted through the papers stacked up on a shelf. In one of the drawers I found a phone with a familiar nonsparkling vampire on the cover. I slipped it into my pocket. Mandy would be glad to get it back, even though I suspected it was her phone that had betrayed her.

"Here," said Brian. He'd found a brochure with a map in it.

There were residences and the cafeteria on one side of the school. The classrooms, offices, and library were on the other side. Next to the library was the faculty lounge, and on the other side of the lounge was a room called the Reflection Center. Mandy had said if she got caught, they'd put her in the "RC." Was that the Reflection Center? Maybe that was a fancy way of saying solitary confinement.

"I think I know where Mandy is," I whispered. But the woman outside was still chattering and walking around. There were more footsteps and voices, sounding more like teenagers. Maybe they'd put together a search party to comb the school.

I fiddled with Mandy's phone to kill time. I figured out how to open the little Web browser and found a play-by-play of the Pats game.

Every time I thought the coast might be clear, there'd be footsteps, or voices, or a door opening. This place sure was busy for a school on a Sunday. Shouldn't everybody be studying quietly in their rooms, or something?

The windows faced east, and the room filled up with shadows, but we didn't dare turn on the lights. I watched the game updates until the screen started to dim, then I shut off the phone to save whatever was left of the battery.

It finally fell quiet outside of the office. I counted to one hundred, just to be sure.

"Let's go," I said. I opened the door and peered out. All the lights were off. That was a good sign.

If I was right about the RC, it was more or less overhead. It was also far from the dorms and cafeteria, which made things easier for us. We crept out of the office, tiptoeing down the hall and up the stairs. The school looked even more like Hogwarts in the dark, with long shadows looming around every corridor.

I saw the sign for the library and stopped, gesturing at Brian to get the door open. He tried a bunch of keys until he found the right one, and we went in. There were shelves on all the walls, full of books, and a table in the middle. The books had titles like *Sarah Stevens: Young Nurse* and *The Virtues of a Virtuoso*. They sounded as dreadful as the school. No wonder Mandy hated it here.

"This is the library," I said.

"Duh," said Brian.

"Don't 'duh' me," I said. "Be right back." I continued down the hall.

If the map was right, Mandy was two rooms over, but you could only get there through the faculty lounge. The doors to the lounge were open, and bright light spilled out into the hallway. It was easy to peek in. There were chairs with high backs and no arms, little round tables with whorls for feet. It looked like a room where old ladies would drink tea. To the right was the door to the Reflection Center. There was a woman about forty years old in front of the door, reading a book with the silhouette of a cat on the cover. The door didn't have bars or anything, but it looked sturdy, and the lock was probably a dead bolt. I knew Mandy would be in trouble, but I didn't expect her to be locked up and under guard like a prisoner.

There were windows along the wall, looking out at rooftops. There was one in the library, too, and maybe even one in the Reflection Center. Maybe I could climb out on the window ledge and creep all the way over to Mandy?

I went back to the library and checked out the window. It didn't open all the way, but it did have a hinged wing that opened a few inches.

"Give me your shoelaces," I told Brian.

"What?"

"I'll give 'em back."

We both kicked off our shoes and unlaced them. I tied the ends together to make a rope.

"That's not long enough to climb down," said Brian.

"Duh."

"Don't 'duh' me either," he said.

I slipped one end of a lace through a notch on the phone, made another knot, and went to the window. I opened it as far as I could and tried to look to the right. I couldn't see the next window over, but that was fine. It meant nobody could see our window from that one.

I turned the phone on, clicked the YouTube app, and searched for kittens. There was a perfect one called "Angry Kitten" that was six minutes long. I put the volume all the way up on the phone.

"Click play, then drop this out and swing it over that way," I told Brian. I handed him the phone and the other end of the makeshift rope.

He took one look at the screen and knew what I was up to. "Got it."

"I need the keys," I said.

He handed them to me. I slipped out of the library into the hall, peeking into the lounge. The woman sat up straight when she heard the sound outside the window, then set her book down and went over. She cranked open the window wing to peer out. "Hi, honey baby. How did you get up there? Come over so I can see you, sweetheart."

I stepped over to the door of the Reflection Center, flipping quietly through the keys. How did Mom keep them straight? There were twenty keys, easy, and no labels. I sorted through and found five or six that looked the right size, then crept over and tried them each in turn. None of them worked. The woman was still squatting by the window.

Her own keys were on the table by her chair, marking her place in her book. I'd have to come within a few inches of her. Now I was glad I'd taken off my shoes.

I tiptoed over and slid out the keys.

"Come on, baby," the woman pleaded. "Let me see you."

I got the door open a second later. Mandy was lying on a bed, her cheeks flushed. She looked at me in shock, wiping at her face with her shirtsleeve. I gestured with my thumb that we were leaving. She nodded and we left, tiptoeing past the guard, who was still kneeling and begging the kitten to come closer. She patted her pockets, like she might have tuna-flavored snacks she'd forgotten about.

We sprinted across the lounge to the hall, passing the library, and I realized I hadn't shut the door to the Reflection Center. As soon as that woman turned around, we were sunk.

"Come on," I told Brian.

It took him a second to reel in the phone.

"The battery is dead," he said. "That was *me* meowing the last five minutes."

"Let's go!" I ran to the end of the hall, tore down the stairs, and threw myself at the first door I saw. It opened, and I felt a brief flash of victory before I remembered that there was a big, unclimbable fence between us and freedom.

Chapter 17 THE OLD SEWER

Mandy was a few steps behind and nearly crashed into me. I heard a loud squeal from inside as Brian came out a second later—the alarm had gone off.

"I lost my shoes on the stairs," he said. "No laces."

Great. We were three runaways without one pair of shoes between us.

"Mandy, how did you get past the fence before?" I asked.

"The old sewer." She took off running and I tried to keep up. Old sewer? I was hoping I'd misheard her.

She ran around the school to a gray, windowless door.

"Locked," she said, yanking on it. I pulled out the keys and started trying them.

"Hurry," said Mandy. "It might say 'Yale' on it because the lock does."

"Oh, yeah, thanks." I tried a few more keys. One went in and didn't turn, but it was close. I scanned the other keys, looking for one that was similar. I found it and got the door open. The alarm was still shrieking. The three of us nearly fell over each other getting in, and Brian pulled the door shut behind us.

Mandy flew down a flight of concrete steps and through a door. She flipped on a light switch. I saw a row of washers and dryers and a couple of metal tables. There was a cart-style laundry basket full of socks and stuff.

"Grab some extra socks," Mandy said. "Two or three pairs."

"I don't want to wear those," said Brian. "They're girl socks."

"Man up," I told him, tossing a handful his way and stooping to put a couple on each of my own feet.

"I'm *not* wearing the ones with pink pom-poms," said Brian, tossing a couple back.

"So where's this sewer?" I asked Mandy. I didn't know how much time we had, but it couldn't be long before people came through that door.

"It's this way," said Mandy. She went past the machines through a doorway and into a cramped area with a bunch of pipes and a humming water heater. "Here," she said, crouching at an access panel in the wall. "This lock is broken." She slipped her fingertips into the space around the panel and pulled it off, exposing a cobwebby crawl space. A moment later she was crawling off into the darkness.

"Gross," said Brian, but he clambered in and followed Mandy.

I was left with the task of getting the panel back into place, which wasn't easy. I used my stubby fingernails to bring the edge of the panel flush with the wall, but I was afraid it would fall if I let go. I waited, breathing in the cobwebs, feeling itchy and tickled all over, trying to hear

147

if anyone was out there. I finally risked pulling my hands back, away from the plate—it stayed put. I crawled off after Mandy and Brian.

The crawl space went ten feet to a drop-off.

"Hello?" I called out. We were in complete blackness.

"Just drop," said Mandy. "It's only a few feet."

I twisted around and backed off the ledge, dropping to a cement floor with a twinge in my ankles. A moment later I heard the clang of the metal plate falling onto the laundry room floor. Somebody would find it and figure out how we escaped, but hopefully we'd be long gone by then.

"What is this place?" Brian asked, his voice echoing against the walls.

"The old sewer," Mandy's voice echoed. She sounded farther away. I heard a click. "Drat! The battery is dead."

"Maybe it's for the best," I told her. "I think they tracked you down through the phone."

"Nobody knows I have it," she said. "It's totally safe."

"They did track you down, though. And I heard my mom say something about it just before—"

"Crud!" She hurled the phone against the cement wall, and we heard it clatter in the dark. "Double crud," she said. "I shouldn't have done that. I'll never find it in here."

"It's probably broke anyway," Brian said. I think he was trying to be helpful.

"It probably *was* my phone," said Mandy. "I was at the library all day, but I went out to call my parents and tell them I was still fine. I was hoping nobody would be home on a Saturday afternoon and I could just leave a message, and nobody was. The police showed up before I could finish. I thought somebody at the library saw me."

"Come on—let's get out of here," I said. "Do we just keep going straight?"

"Yeah," she said. "At least we can't get lost in here. It's just one big tube."

There was only a trickle of water, but my feet got damp and cold right away, even with all the socks. The pipe was big, but I had to walk hunched over, and my back started to ache.

"This sewer hasn't been used in a hundred years," Mandy said when we were farther along in the darkness. "I looked up a building abstract on the state housing website, then did some creative Googling to find out the original plans, which are part of the architectural library at Columbia University. I had to chat up this geeky college student to get a log-in to their digital repository, but I finally got the blueprint. This was somebody's house before it was a school, and it had its own water system. Eventually the owners tapped into the town's water supply, because it existed by then. But the old system was still here. It was pointed the wrong way for the town's sewer system, but nobody's ever filled it in. They never capped it either, or I would have had to turn around and go back."

"How did you even know to *look* for that?" I asked her.

"I didn't know what I was looking for," she said. "I got the idea from Sherlock Holmes. Actually, his older, smarter brother."

"He has one?" Brian asked.

"Yes. Mycroft Holmes. He never goes outside, but there's a story where he solves a mystery by looking at a blueprint for a building. When I read that, I got the idea to find the blueprint for the school and see if there was anything I could use."

We reached the end of the sewer pipe and stepped into a shallow gully among thick brush. There was a glimmer of late afternoon visible above the trees, but it would be dark soon. Evening comes fast in the woods.

The ditch probably used to be a creek, and that was where the rich people dumped their sewage. Lovely people.

"That wasn't fun," I said, stretching. It felt great after being hunched up in the pipe.

"I thought it was fun," said Brian.

"Hey, we got lucky this time," Mandy said. "Last time I saw a possum or something in the tunnel."

"Aw, I missed it," said Brian.

"Well, thanks for rescuing me," said Mandy. "What now?"

"I don't know," I admitted. I'd planned on talking to Mandy and biking home, not walking through a sewer pipe and getting dumped off in the middle of the woods. "I didn't plan on rescuing you. I just thought I'd talk to you."

"I was going to rescue you!" said Brian. "And I'm the one who did, because Eric didn't even bring keys or anything. He wouldn't have even gotten inside, I bet."

"So what was *your* plan?" I asked him.

"To go back to Michelle's house," he said, then clapped a hand over his mouth.

"Michelle's home now," I told him. "And I already figured out what happened, so don't worry about it."

"You told!" said Brian. I was confused until I realized he was talking to Mandy.

"I didn't tell him anything. He just figured it out," she said. "I'll start calling him Mycroft. He's your older, smarter brother."

"Oh, come on," I said. It wasn't that hard to put the pieces together.

"She was going to sleep in the woods," said Brian. "That's the only reason I told her."

"Oh, I would have figured out *something*," said Mandy.

When was Mandy going to sleep in the woods? What did Brian tell her? I'd just assumed they'd met at Michelle's the day after my accident.

"I didn't mean to tell her anything," said Brian. "I didn't even know she was a runaway. She just asked me if I'd seen some glowing mushrooms, so I showed her where they were and we were talking, and I told her about Cassie and how Michelle was going to take photographs of bears. . . ."

"Forget it," I said. I couldn't process half of what they were saying, and it didn't matter. However they met, we were still stuck in the woods now, with no shoes and no way home. I would never find my bike in this darkness, and Brian's was too close to the front gate of the school. We couldn't risk searching for it, and we couldn't all three ride on his little bike.

"I guess we'll have to walk home," I said. "It'll take about two hours."

"It took me three hours before," said Mandy. "And that was in the daytime. And I had shoes."

"Which way is it?" Brian asked.

"That way." I pointed north. You could see the glimmer of blue-green mushroom light hovering above the treetops in the distance.

"Wow," Mandy said in a whisper. "It's kind of amazing."

"At least they're good for something," I said.

We found the trail to Boise Township and started walking. It was easy to lose track of the trail in the dark, and we had to stop sometimes to pick out the pine needles that had worked their way into our socks. It was a downright miserable hike.

I puzzled over what Brian and Mandy had just been talking about. He'd showed her the mushrooms, but when? By the time I'd met Mandy, they weren't hard to find, but that was a couple of days after she ran away. She must have met Brian first. Brian had been off in the woods that afternoon, after the haunted house.

It was clear now: Mandy met Brian and asked him if he'd seen the glowing mushrooms. He took her to them, babbling like Brian does sometimes, and tipped Mandy off about Michelle's vacant house—the easiest house in town for a stranger to find, because it was the one with a pig. She found the house, found the key, and let herself in. It was no big deal, but I was impressed Brian was able to keep the whole thing a secret. For a kid who couldn't shut up, he could keep a secret.

"I'm hungry," said Brian.

"You think you're hungry?" I said. "What about me?"

"I'm more tired than hungry," said Mandy.

We weren't even halfway home, and the second leg would be harder than the first.

"Keep on keeping on," I said.

"Okay, Coach," said Mandy.

We walked on toward the blue-green light until we heard a low, growly noise in the distance.

"Great. It's a bear," said Brian.

"Or maybe a moose," I said. "Either way, I'm eating it."

"Moose don't growl," said Mandy.

"How do you know? Have you ever heard one?"

A moment later a machine broke through the trees. It was about a hundred years old, with high, narrow tires and a blocky frame. It looked like a prehistoric ATV. Perched on top, wearing aviator glasses and white leather gloves, was an old woman waving a flashlight. She nudged the goggles back, and I recognized her immediately.

It was the witch.

Chapter 18 THE WITCH'S MACHINE

It was the witch from the haunted house, the creepy way-too-believable one who had scared me to tears when I was a little kid. She had to be a real witch, too, showing up in the middle of the woods at night on a contraption that looked like she'd made it with witch magic out of a stove and a baby carriage.

"You ran away from the school," she said. She pointed the flashlight beam in Mandy's face, then in Brian's. "You didn't. They don't take boys." She came to me last, the light lingering on my face. I squinted against the light. "You look familiar. Do you work at the five-and-dime?"

"No," I said. "I'm from Tanglewood."

"I just went up to look at your mushrooms," she said. "Read about them in the newspaper and decided to go see."

"The newspaper said they'll go away after the first frost."

"They probably will," she said. "I don't think I ever saw mushrooms after a frost. Anyway, if you don't want to be lost anymore, you can come to my house. I can only take one of you on the quad, but it's not far."

"Um. No thanks," Mandy told her.

"Me too," I agreed.

"I'll go," said Brian. He climbed up in the seat before I could stop him.

"Come on, Bri. We don't even know this person."

"She's just an old lady," said Brian.

"If you two want stew and shoes, follow the quad." The witch cranked the wheel to get her machine turned around, and chugged on into the woods.

"Brian, get back here!"

He didn't. There was nothing to do but hurry after them, following the single red taillight through the dark, stumbling over stones and roots as we tried to keep up.

Mandy tripped and went sprawling, and I turned back to help. By the time I'd helped her up, the red light had vanished. We followed the trail for another quarter of a mile before we landed in the backyard of a clapboard house.

"I'm getting a *Blair Witch* vibe from this whole thing," Mandy said.

"Seriously," I agreed, although I'd never heard of that particular witch. "I half expected the house to be made of gingerbread."

We went up the steps and found the back door open. Brian was at the kitchen table, and the witch lady was spooning coffee into a kettle.

"Borrow some shoes if you want," she said. She pointed at a row of L.L.Bean boots. "I buy up factory seconds at the outlet store. I want one pair for every kind of Maine weather, but I still need a dozen more to get through the average day." She cackled at her own joke. The cackling was not helping me think of her as a harmless old woman and not a witch. I wanted to check out the cupboards to see if she had a lot of eyes of newt and powdered bat wings.

Brian was already wearing some snow mocs that looked comfy but also girly, with a ruff of fleece around the ankle.

"You might as well be wearing the pink pom-pom socks," I said. He ignored me.

I found a pair of plain brown boots that were probably lady boots too, but they fit okay. Mandy took a pair of waders that went up to her knees.

"Going fly-fishing?" I asked her.

"I think they're stylin'," she said.

"I want all those boots back," the old woman said.

"Of course."

The coffee kettle started gurgling, and the woman opened the cupboard. That was my chance to snoop, but all I saw were rows and rows of Maggie Dunne beef stew. The woman opened two and dumped them into a pot, then added a can or so of tap water.

"This is an old family recipe," she said with a cackle. I wished she'd stop cackling. I was glad that she wasn't bustling about adding pinches of this and that from mysterious jars, anyway—the stew was probably safe.

"So how did you get out of the Llewellan place?" she asked Mandy.

"The what place?" Brian asked around a mouthful of cracker. He'd been digging into a box of saltines.

"She means Alden," said Mandy. "That's who the mansion belonged to, way back when."

Brian didn't die on the spot, so I took a couple of crackers myself.

"I started as the Llewellans' cook at the end of World War II and stayed on as the school cook after the place changed hands. They made me retire in the 1990s, so I must have been there almost forty years."

"It's more like *fifty* years," said Mandy.

"Well, I never was good with numbers." She got a bright blue flame going on the stove and stirred the stew a little. "Did you escape through the old sewer pipe?"

"How did you guess?" Mandy asked.

"Girls used to come and go through that thing all the time. They'd meet boys as far away as Portland and still get back before daybreak. I never told anyone. Figured it wasn't my business to tell them anything if it wasn't about the kitchen."

She looked at the coffee kettle, saw it was still gurgling, and stirred the stew some more. "You picked a strange way to do it, though, walking through an old sewer with no shoes."

"It wasn't exactly planned," Mandy explained.

The coffee and stew had the same thickness when she was done, but I gobbled up my bowl in less than a minute. It wasn't great, but it was made of food, and that was good enough for me. I wondered if this was the sort of thing she made when she was a cook at that school, or if she got so sick of cooking she went for the easy stuff now.

"What's that thing you were driving?" I asked her. "It's cool."

"It's mostly a Royal Enfield quadricycle, but it's got a

new motor from a 1955 Enfield Bullet. Plus a few other parts here and there. It gets me around."

"It reminds me of *Chitty Chitty Bang Bang*," said Mandy.

"It's the only wheels I have anymore," the old woman said. "Thank heavens Sylvester left it for me."

"Was that your husband?" Mandy asked.

"Nah, this old coot who lived here before I did. I bought it back in nineteen . . ." She screwed up her face. "Well, it was after Pa died and before the Llewellan place got turned into a school."

Brian started yawning, and for a moment I worried that we'd all made a bad mistake—that the stew was laced with something after all, or maybe the coffee, and now we'd all three go to sleep and wake up in cages. But the woman had eaten the same stew and drunk the same coffee as we did, and besides that, I felt fine.

"Can you tell me where the, uh . . . ," Mandy started to ask. The woman nodded and pointed her to a door. "Through there and to the right."

Brian pushed his bowl aside, propped his head up with his hand, and snoozed. Mandy was gone a long time. I wasn't sure how long, exactly, but it felt long and I started to get worried again. The old woman bustled about like nothing was wrong, washing the dishes (I should have offered to do them, I realized—a weird thought in the middle of wondering whether she was trying to kill us all), then poured another cup of coffee.

"I have to wash up too," I told her. I got up and went through another room that led to the bathroom. It was one big room that looked like it was part living room, part office, part dining room, and part attic—it was the combination of a couch, a desk and shelves, an oval table, and dozens of boxes all over the place.

Mandy was looking with wide eyes at something.

"Hey." I nudged her shoulder, and she pointed, her lips moving but not making a word. It was a built-in bookshelf crammed full of books. There were a few hardbacks, a lot of paperbacks, and a stack of magazines on the bottom shelf. They looked old.

I scanned the spines of the books and saw that every single one was by Max Bailey. I thumbed through the magazines, which had faded cover pictures of monsters or spaceships. They each had a list of authors on the cover, and Max Bailey's name was always among them.

"All rare volumes and first editions," Mandy said in a whisper. "Even the Max Bailey collection at the Portland library doesn't have this much stuff."

"Don't take anything," I whispered back.

"What?" She looked appalled that I would even suggest such a thing.

"Well, you do steal stuff sometimes," I pointed out.

"Nothing like this," she whispered back. "Nothing valuable."

"Ah, you've found the books." The woman came to the door. "I don't even read that stuff. I think life is scary enough without making up ghosts and monsters."

"Then why do you *have* them?" Mandy asked. "Did Sylvester leave these, too?"

"Nah, those were my pa's."

"This collection is worth a lot. Seriously. You could sell them. Or donate them to a library. Share them with the world."

"I didn't say I didn't want them," the woman said. "I said I didn't *read* them."

Mandy looked flustered, disappointed, and cross all at the same time.

"They were my pa's," the woman explained. "They mean a lot to me."

"Wow, he must have been a really big Max Bailey fan," said Mandy.

"Um, I think her father *was* Max Bailey," I said.

"Oh!" Mandy turned and looked, and the woman nodded.

"He may have written scary stuff, but he was a good man," she said.

"I know," said Mandy hoarsely.

"Is your name Howard?" I asked her. The biography I'd read said Max Bailey had one child. I'd thought it was a mistake in the book when they said it was a daughter.

"Yep. Pa's two favorite writer pals were both named Howard, so he had that name all picked out for his first son. When Ma died in childbirth, he didn't know if there'd ever be another wife or a son in his life, so he named me Howard."

"I'm sorry," I told her.

"About my name or my ma?"

"Both, I guess."

"Well, I didn't even know Howard was a boy's name until I was in school," she said. "I'll never forget how my first teacher hollered at me for being a sass, asking my real name again and again until I finally gave up and stormed out of the room. That set the tone for me all the way through school." She laughed the way she did sometimes. It didn't sound like a cackle to me anymore. It was more like a dry laugh.

"In case you couldn't tell, I love your father's work," Mandy said. "Seriously. He's amazing."

"Thank you. I don't think he expected folks to even know who he was this many years later, but I'm glad they do."

"You have all the books but not any of his pictures," I said. I liked the pictures better.

"I sold them off, over the years," she said. "The school didn't have much of a retirement program, so it was a lifesaver. Sold the last one for a good sum. Though I hear it's worth ten times that now. I never could part with his books, though."

"Do people pester you a lot?" Mandy asked. "Your father has . . . well, he has some crazy big fans."

"Ah, they used to track me down," said Howard. "Someone writing a biography, or hoping to dig up a long-lost manuscript. It's been years since anyone did that, though. Maybe everyone thinks I'm dead—I don't know."

"Is there a long-lost manuscript?" Mandy asked hopefully.

"You know, he asked me to burn his manuscripts after he died. All the drafts and unfinished works."

"I know he asked, but—did you go through with it?"

"No, I didn't. I always told him he'd have to do it himself. I wouldn't burn up anyone's hard work, especially his."

Mandy closed her eyes and wobbled a little bit. I thought she might actually faint.

"Before you ask, though," Howard told her, "no, you can't read it, and it's not even because I won't let you, although I wouldn't anyway."

"Huh?"

"I got to where I didn't trust these fellows who were sniffing around, so I put everything in a safe about twenty-five years ago." She counted out decades on her fingers. "Maybe it was thirty-five years ago. However long ago it was, I lost the combination somewhere in between then and now and haven't been able to open it since. I can't even blast it open, because I might burn the papers."

"Did you set the combination yourself?" Mandy asked her. "Because if you did, maybe we can figure it out. Birthdays, lucky numbers . . ."

"I did set it myself, but I tried all of those a hundred times each. I don't know what was on my mind. I have no head for numbers and never did."

"Maybe we could help you remember," Mandy said.

"Ha!" Howard laughed. "You think looking for a needle in a haystack is hard, try looking in this muddled brain of mine for numbers."

"You would have picked something you'd remember," said Mandy. "I mean, something you thought you'd remember."

"Yeah, well, I've forgotten about half of what I remember," said Howard.

I glanced at a clock on the wall. "I wish I could help, but Brian and I better go home."

"Want to take the quad?" Howard asked. "I'm too tired to go on a drive, but if you bring it back first thing tomorrow, I suppose you can borrow it."

"Seriously?" An hour ago I'd thought she was a witch, and here she'd given us all food and shoes and now was lending me her only wheels.

"You can't take it," Mandy whispered, "Don't. It's too much."

"You seemed to like it," said Howard. "You might as well give it a spin." She took me outside to show me how to start the quad.

I had a hard time at first, pumping the clutch and revving the motor at the right time. Finally a few puffs of heavy black smoke came out and the motor sputtered to life. The clutch, throttle, and brake were all pedals, and it took me a while to get used to them and remember which was which. I lurched in circles around the yard until I got the hang of it.

"I have to go get my brother," I said. I'd left him sleeping at the kitchen table.

"You know, I always felt bad about the haunted house," she told me as we walked back to the house. "I didn't realize how young you were. I never meant to set you off."

"You remember that?"

"I got kicked out of the haunted house for it," she said. "So yeah, I remember."

"Wow. I'm sorry too, then. I didn't mean to get you in trouble."

"They said I was too scary for kids," she said. "Can you believe that? I mean, don't they try to make the house scary?"

"Yeah," I admitted. "Well, maybe scaring people too well runs in your family?"

"Maybe so. I hope this makes up for scaring the tarnation out of you."

"Way more," I said.

Brian was waking up. He made a big noisy yawn and rubbed the sleep out of his eyes. "Do we get to go back on the thing?"

"Yep."

"Awesome."

"You can stay here for a while," Howard told Mandy. "I won't tell on you. I never liked the way that school pushed girls around."

"That's really nice," said Mandy. "Thanks."

"Yeah," I agreed.

"Maybe you can rummage around in my brain tomorrow and find that combination," Howard told her. "If you don't mind the dust and cobwebs."

Chapter 19 LOST IN THE WOODS

We found the trail back to Tanglewood, the mushroom light growing brighter and brighter as we got closer. The quad only went about eight miles an hour, and the steering was easy—you used handlebars like you would with a bike. It was fun once we got used to bouncing around.

Soon we were cruising along the mushroom caps, and it was an even slower and bouncier ride, but the bounces were less jarring. It was like riding on Jell-O. I slowed down as I got close to Tanglewood. We could hear voices and footsteps along the trails—fewer people than last night, but still plenty of gawkers.

I tried to avoid them but nearly ran over some guy in a Colby College sweatshirt. I slammed on the brakes just before he got flattened. A woman I assumed was his girlfriend stood just off the trail.

"Wow, what is that thing?" the guy asked.

"It's a quadricycle," said Brian. "Don't you college kids know *anything?*"

The guy's girlfriend laughed. "He told you, Brendan!"

"Of course I've heard of quartercycles," he said. "I just never saw one like that."

I blasted by them but slowed way down when we were nearly home. I wasn't too eager to get there. We'd been gone for a really long time, and I didn't even have a bag of Fritos to show for it.

Brian was quiet until I brought the quad to a stop at the edge of the woods.

"That was the most fun ever," he said. "Can we do it again?"

"Well, we have to take the thing back tomorrow, so sure."

We hid the quad behind the shed and went in through the back door. The kitchen light was on. We took the Bean boots off and put them in the hall closet, then knocked a parka off the hanger to cover them, hoping it looked like ordinary closet mess that nobody would notice or try to clean up. We'd barely closed the door when Mom came flying out of the kitchen, scooping up Brian.

"Put me down!" he shouted, even though his tiptoes never left the ground.

She squeezed him first, then let him go and hugged me.

"You're all right," she said.

"Yeah," I said, and launched into an explanation before she could get another word in: I'd gone for a ride and blown out a tire. It was a long walk home and I got lost in the woods. Brian was following me and left his bike with mine—I didn't have a good reason for why he'd do that, but she didn't ask for one.

"I'm glad you're both okay, but you couldn't have picked a worse day," she said.

"Sorry."

"No, I'm sorry. It's not your fault. I had another disaster at work, but I didn't go in. I can't handle a missing girl when my own boys are missing." She sniffed. "You know I love you two more than anyone. My job keeps me busy, but I really am doing it all for you. You know that, right?"

"Sure," said Brian. "Another girl is missing?" I could have hugged him for playing it so cool.

"The same girl is missing again." She noticed our feet. "What happened to your shoes?"

"We took them off when we came in. They were really muddy."

"Hm." She squinted at our socks, which were also pretty messy. Too messy for her to tell they were girl socks, at least.

"We need to shower and go to bed," I said, stretching for effect.

"You must be hungry."

"Oh, yeah." We should have been hungry. Actually, I was hungry. That stew already seemed like a long time ago.

"First let me call your father and tell him he can stop looking for you," she said. "Then I'll heat up some of Dad's chili."

She picked up the phone, and we took advantage of the pause to run upstairs. When I went into my room, I saw splashes of blue-green here and there in the darkness. There were mushrooms dotting the walls. The fungus must have scaled the exterior of our house, wiggling through the woodwork and poking through the plaster.

• • •

After second supper I went to bed, leaving the lights on. I'd rather have regular light than the patches of neon. I fell asleep right away, but a second later Dad woke me up.

"Are you afraid of the dark now?"

"No, just the stuff that hides in it." It was a joke we used to make when I was little. "Dad, the house is in really bad shape."

"I know," he said. "I ran into the Shop Smart tonight, but they were out of every brand of fungal spray and powder. I'll try some more places tomorrow. I'll drive to Bangor if I have to."

"Okay," I said. I doubted a spray would do it, but at least he was finally doing something.

"You missed a good game," he said.

"I know. I'm sorry."

"You don't have to be sorry. It sounds like you had a real adventure today."

"Yep."

"Maybe you and Brian shouldn't go to school tomorrow," he said. "The doctor said you should rest up, and you really haven't."

"Yeah," I agreed. "I mean, yeah, I could use a day of rest."

I got up before anybody else, put on my loafers because my sneakers were long gone, and tapped on Brian's door.

"Are you up?" I whispered.

"Yeah."

"We have to return the quad and get our bikes."

After a quick breakfast, we grabbed the Bean boots and left the house. The mushrooms were eight or nine inches tall, coating the deck and rails and scaling the side of the house like ivy. They shone dimly in the morning light.

"Can I drive this time?" Brian pleaded. "Please?"

"No."

I went to the shed, which was now a bluish-lit den and smelled like rotten wood. Tendrils of fungus were working their way through the thin wood of the shed walls. I grabbed a tank of gas that we kept for the lawn mower and snowblower and slammed the shed door.

I topped off the tank of the quad with gas but then had trouble starting it.

"Let me try," said Brian.

"No."

I rummaged through a compartment on the quad between the seats, looking for instructions. I didn't find any, but I did find a little bottle of lead additive for gasoline. Of course—gas was different way back when this contraption was made.

After I added a little of the liquid to the tank, the engine started right up, puffing black toxic smoke into the clean morning air. This thing has got to be bad for the environment, I thought. Why did everything good in life have to be bad for somebody or something?

I headed south, picking up the trail to go to Howard's. I stopped by the big rock I'd tipped over. From there I could see the black circle of death in the woods. It was bigger than the last time I saw it, and the smell of decaying wood was overwhelming.

"It's worse," said Brian.

"I know."

I revved the motor and hurried on. By "hurried," I mean cranked it up to maybe ten miles an hour—a lawn tractor could outrace it. I followed a trail that went west, deeper into the woods, gradually arcing south. I took some of the hills kind of hard, to make the ride bouncier, and Brian yelped every time.

We realized it was pretty early to bang on someone's door, so we left the quad in the yard and the boots on the back porch and went off to find our bikes.

"They probably found our shoes by now," Brian said as we walked. "Mom will see them and know they're ours."

"Maybe." My Puma sneaks were pretty common, and I'd bought them with my pig-sitting money. I wasn't sure Mom noticed what kind of sports shoes I wore. Could police take toe prints off the inside toe? Or would they even need to, since our fingerprints were on them too?

"Why did you want to rescue Mandy?" Brian asked.

"I told you, I didn't mean to," I told him. "I just wanted to talk to her. What about you? So Dad would stay here longer?"

"I like her," said Brian.

"I like her too, but I didn't plan to bust her out," I said. "The school stinks, but you know—she needs a place to live. And her parents need to know she's all right."

We went off the trail so we wouldn't get too close to Alden.

"We didn't tell Mom and Dad where we went yesterday," said Brian. "They didn't know if we were all right."

"Stop being logical."

We found Brian's bike right away, but I had trouble finding my own.

"Maybe they searched the area and found it," said Brian.

"Maybe so," I said. If so, I was done for. The bike had a number hidden on the frame, to prove it belonged to me if it ever got stolen. It probably also proved that I belonged to the bike. But I figured if they didn't find Brian's, they couldn't have looked very hard.

Fortunately we did find it, stashed farther off the trail than I remembered and well hidden. I entered the combination, which was 9797—my football number twice over. If Howard had as much imagination as I did setting combinations, Mandy would have cracked that safe open in three seconds.

Chapter 20 WHEN EVERYTHING ELSE IS GONE

Howard was on the couch holding her head. Some blankets were bunched up at the other end. Mandy was sitting on the floor by the safe with a notebook and a pen, surrounded by boxes that had been shoved out of the way.

"Maybe it was the days of the month your grandparents were born," she suggested.

"Didn't you try all four combinations using those numbers?" Howard asked.

"There are *twenty-four* combinations," said Mandy. "And I did try them all, but that was when we still thought your grandfather was born on the twenty-first, but according to the obituary we found, he was born on the twelfth."

"I told you that was a mistake."

"But maybe you went with the typo?"

"Now why would I do that?" Howard asked. "Oh, hello," she said, finally noticing us standing there in the doorway. "I'm letting this girl give me the third, fourth, and fifth degrees."

"I just want to help," said Mandy.

"I know, I know. I told you it was no use. I've been

172

through the whole family tree and tried all the birth dates, death dates, and wedding dates in every order. I've been through all my favorite books and songs in search of numbers. Whatever it was I thought I'd remember is long gone. Anyway, I'm getting hungry." She got up. "Anyone want lunch?"

"Sure," I said. Brian nodded, a little unsurely. Mandy didn't seem to notice the question. She was still fiddling with the dial on the safe.

Brian crouched to thumb through the magazines on the bottom of the bookshelf, settling on one with a giant robot on it.

"Can I read this?" he asked, showing it to Howard.

"Just be careful with it."

"Thanks!" He followed her into the kitchen carrying the magazine. I caught a flash of Max Bailey's mushroom monster on the back cover.

"I read this book once about a safecracker who used a stethoscope to listen to the tumblers," Mandy said. "I wonder if that really works. And I wonder where I could find a stethoscope."

"The doctor store?" I suggested.

"Is there one?"

"I don't know." I noticed a huge, careening pile of Bangor newspapers next to the safe. Yesterday's was on top.

"You should read this," I told Mandy, grabbing the paper and showing her the headline: AN EERIE AUTUMN. "It says there was a similar outbreak of mushrooms eighty years ago."

"We knew that," she said. "I found a newspaper article from back then, remember?"

"That one didn't say where they were or how many there were. This says they were right here, and that there were a lot of them, and that it could even be the same fungus. I don't mean the same *kind* of fungus, but the exact same one. It doesn't die. It just kind of hibernates."

She took the newspaper and skimmed the article. "It doesn't even say what happened to them." She dropped the paper back on the pile. "It's useless."

"You've been doing all that research," I said. "I was hoping you'd know what to do."

"I don't," she said, "but I do know what to *ask*."

"Don't go all Yoda on me."

"First, what happened to those mushrooms eighty years ago?"

"That's what I want to know."

"Second, why is the Keatston Meetinghouse around when everything else is gone?"

"I don't know. I don't think anybody does."

"If we find out, we can save it again," she said. "And maybe the rest of the town along with it."

Howard was at the stove mixing up a batch of Maggie Dunne beef stew. Two cans were sitting on the counter, gravy dripping down the edges and smudging the face of the kid on the can. She started ladling the stew into four bowls. Brian folded the magazine and set it on the pantry shelf behind him so he wouldn't get food on it.

How old was Howard? She said she started working

at the end of World War II, which was 1940-something. I should have paid more attention in history class. Anyway, she probably did remember what happened, especially if it had a big effect on her dad.

"You rode up to see the mushrooms yesterday?" I said as soon as the stew was served. I wanted to work my way around to the real question.

"Yep. They're something."

"Have you seen anything like them before?" I asked.

"Mmm . . ." She was either mulling it over or enjoying her food. "Do you know what a mycologist is?" she finally asked.

"Someone who studies mushrooms," Mandy said.

"Well, I'm not one," said Howard. "I've seen lots of mushrooms, and since I never liked eating them, I never paid much attention to one kind versus another."

That ended the discussion. I suspected she knew more than she was letting on.

I was scraping my bowl before anyone else was halfway finished. I wanted to help out a bit, so I got up and washed the pot and sponged the gravy off the stove. I saw the cans sitting there all goopy and rinsed them out in the sink so I could throw them in the recycle bin.

Brian jumped up from the table and grabbed one of the cans from me. "I have an idea!" he shouted. He darted out of the room with the can.

"Is there sugar in this stuff?" Mandy asked. "He seems a little hyper."

"I don't know," said Howard. "Check the ingredients."

Brian came back into the room and set the dripping can in the middle of the table like a centerpiece.

"I opened the safe!" he said. "The combination is fifteen five nineteen thirty-seven."

"That was it!" Howard pounded the table with her fist, rattling the bowls. "Maggie Dunne beef stew. Fifteen point five ounces in each and every can. I've been looking at it every day for years and forgot that it had anything to do with anything."

I picked up the can and read the banner under the kid's face: "Since nineteen thirty-seven. Sixty years of goodness!" They reached sixty years of goodness the year I was born. I hoped that they just never got around to updating the label, instead of the can being that old.

"That's pretty incredible thinking," Mandy told Brian. "You should switch around the *a* and the *i* in your name."

"I saw the cans and thought that might be it." Brian was lit up like a glowing mushroom.

"Good work," I told him. "Now eat your stew."

"So what do you do now?" I asked Mandy when we were cleaning up after lunch. Brian had earned his way out of cleaning up and was at the table turning the pages in the magazine, mostly looking at the pictures.

"I'm going to look at the lost manuscripts of Max Bailey," she said. "What do you think? This is the most incredible thing that's ever happened to me."

"I thought you were going to help me with the mushroom problem."

"I *am* helping," she said. "It's all connected, Eric. Max Bailey is what got me interested in it in the first place. The answer might be right there in that safe."

"Yeah, right." I handed her the last washed dish to dry.

"Give me a day or two," she said. "The mushrooms aren't going anywhere."

"Yeah they are. They're going *everywhere*."

We finished up and went into the other room. Howard had moved the stacks of papers out of the safe, making a tower that looked ready to capsize.

"I'm afraid these are in no kind of order," she said, "and I don't have the eyesight or the patience to straighten this mess out."

"We can help!" Mandy practically shouted.

"I'd rather you didn't read any more than you have to," she said. "My pa asked me to burn it all, and I didn't. But I never showed any of it to anyone either. That was a compromise I made with myself."

"We'll be good," said Mandy.

The sooner the papers were put together and locked away, the sooner Mandy would get back to the mushroom issue. I decided to help out.

It was more than I bargained for, though. Most of the pages didn't have titles or page numbers, and they were shuffled together in no particular order. We worked on the floor. I took out the papers that did have titles and numbers at the top, because those were the easiest to deal with. The papers were yellowed at the edges and brittle. They were all short stories, with titles like "The Phantom of Portland" and "The

Stalking Dread." I knew some of the titles from the book, so not all of these stories were unpublished. The original drafts were still probably a big deal. I didn't have any paper clips or folders, so I stacked them crisscross style.

Mandy had a slower job but the one she wanted—she had to read the bottoms of untitled, unnumbered pages and then find the tops that came next. She had little stacks of twos and threes slowly coming together like a jigsaw puzzle.

Howard took anything that looked personal—letters and journals and contracts—over to the couch. Sometimes she would mutter to herself or sigh as she read.

"I'm bored," Brian said after we'd been at it for a while. He'd been sitting by the bookshelf, thumbing through more old magazines. I'd forgotten about him. "Ms. Bailey, can I please drive that quad thing?"

"How old are you?" asked Howard. She'd been reading a wide book with tiny handwriting across the pages. It looked like what I imagined ship logs looked like, but it must have been Max Bailey's diary.

"Ten," he lied. "I mean eleven. I just had a birthday and forgot."

"He's nine for another month," I said. I didn't think Brian should cruise around the woods on the quad by himself.

"What if I take you for a ride?" Howard offered Brian. "I could use some air myself." She set her book on the coffee table so she could go show him how to use the quad.

"Okay!"

"Look," Mandy said as soon as they were gone. She shoved a piece of paper at me. It looked like the first page of a story, a title halfway down the page:

THE FUNGAL WRATH

"It's the long-lost story," she whispered.
"Yeah," I whispered back. "I guessed that from the title."
"Read the first sentence."
I did, and read it twice more to make sure I wasn't losing my mind:

```
At long last, it is time to record
the    terrible    occurrence    at    the
village   of   Keatston,   Maine,   which
left  no  survivors  and  few  clues  to
what happened.
```

"It's about Keatston," I said.
"I told you that the answer was in this safe."
"We don't know that yet." I started to skim the page. "Anyway, it's just a story." Max had come up to see the mushrooms and gotten an idea for a story. We knew that. Maybe he had stopped at the museum—was it a museum back then? Well, he would have seen the Meetinghouse, and somebody would have told him about it.
"Find all the pages," Mandy whispered.
"That's what I'm doing." I skipped to the bottom of

the page and saw the beginning of a sentence: "When he approached . . ."

I shuffled through the pages trying to find one that had something a guy would approach, finding a couple of possibilities. I decided that the guy was approaching "the Royal Governmental Council of the Province of Massachusetts Bay," and not "a dismal house that reeked of mildew," or "a turgid wormlike creature with a ring of razor-sharp teeth and a single, fluid, knowing eyeball." I started looking for the third page, which would finish the sentence "Although they were uncertain of . . ."

"This is going to take forever," I said. "Maybe you can find the last page and we'll work backward and meet in the middle?"

She went through all the pages but shook her head.

"I don't see anything that looks like a last page," she said. "Nothing that says 'The End,' or even ends halfway down the page."

"So maybe it isn't finished?"

"Or maybe the ending is missing."

I worked quickly, finding page after page until I heard the back door closing and Howard coming through the kitchen. I took as much of the manuscript as I'd put together and shoved it under my shirt, and I jumped up just as she entered the room. I stuck my thumbs in the belt loops on my jeans so I could keep the pages from spilling out. It made me feel like a cowboy.

The quad motor was still roaring in the yard.

"Are you letting him drive?" I asked her.

"I said he could do circles in the yard," she said. "I figured he deserved a reward for cracking that safe open."

"I better go check on him. Really, we should get going home anyway. Thanks for lunch."

"You're always welcome," she said.

I hurried outside as best I could with my thumbs in my belt loops, which wasn't fast at all. I guess you could call it moseying.

We biked home on the highway so we wouldn't have to pedal through mushrooms. Even then we had to cut through ridges that spliced the road as we got closer to home. When we put our bikes in the garage, I noticed it was beginning to look as bad as the shed, with mushrooms scaling the walls and making their way across the ceiling.

We found Dad in my bedroom with a bucket of stinky water and a stiff brush, scrubbing the wall. The floor was littered with severed mushroom caps.

"Where were you guys?" he said. "I've been defungifying the house. There were red ones on the stairs!"

"We had to get our bikes," said Brian. "And Eric had to fix his tire. He took me to Firelight for lunch and I had a pork sandwich. Eric had chicken because he doesn't eat pig. I still eat pig but I won't ever eat Cassie."

I put my hand on his shoulder to stop him, but I had to give him credit. The kid knew how to fib.

"Can I go play video games?" he asked.

"Sure," said Dad. Brian ran back downstairs.

"I would have driven you out there," said Dad. "I went

that way anyway, to get this stuff." He showed me a yellow can of antifungal powder. "It's meant for lawns, but it was the best I could do."

"Do you want me to help?"

"You're supposed to be taking it easy, you know. And here you've already been on a long walk and a bike ride."

"Oh, yeah."

"How come your shirt's tucked in?"

"I don't know," I said, looking at my sweatshirt like I hadn't realized that it was.

"You're also wearing your dress shoes," he said.

"I guess so," I said.

"Get some rest," he said. "I can finish this later." He took a minute to sweep up the mushroom caps and left me alone with the smell of something between paint remover and baby powder.

Chapter 21 THE WILDERNESS ABOUNDS WITH MONSTERS

The Max Bailey story was about William Keats, the guy who founded Keatston. He was pretty normal at first, but after his wife died, he started to see the wrong in everything. He saw the wickedness in his friends and stopped hanging out with them. He was a clerk for a Boston shipping company and began to regret plundering the pristine continent for the wealth of the Crown, which was how the story put it, and he wanted to do something holier. So he quit his job and became an emissary for God. I had to look that word up. It meant he was a preacher without a church. He preached outside, like one of those guys you see on street corners in the city.

William Keats believed that America was meant to be holy, but also thought that Boston wasn't a shining city on the hill anymore like it was supposed to be when the Pilgrims founded it, and he decided to start all over again in the wilderness.

Maine was mostly wilderness back then. It was part of Massachusetts, and Massachusetts was part of England. There was a royal council that presided over the colony, and they were handing out land up in Maine to anyone who wanted to live there. The French Canadians were acting like Maine was theirs, and the English figured the way to drive them out of the territory was to move a lot of colonists up there to settle it. So William Keats got some other people together who also thought Boston wasn't shiny enough anymore and asked the council for some land, and they got it.

Sixty-seven people moved with Mr. Keats to Maine, and they built houses and planted potatoes and cabbages and created their holy town in the wilderness. They never called it Keatston themselves, but that's how the council wrote it up in the charter.

That took six or seven pages for Max Bailey to tell, and I already knew most of it. I have to admit he told it better than the folks at the museum. It was less like history and more like real people doing stuff.

William had a son just before his wife died. The baby was barely mentioned in the first part of the story but got more important after they moved up to Maine. His name was Benjamin. He was a big kid and got in a lot of fistfights with other boys. Townspeople said it was the lack of a mother, and that he was growing up without good graces that a mother gives a child. They were sympathetic but also a little scared of Benjamin.

According to the story, Benjamin got more and more sinister. He got a knife somewhere and started using it on people. The whole story became more like a late-night horror flick. He knifed this kid named Alex, and when his dad tried to punish him for it, Benjamin knifed him too. He didn't kill either one of them, but I guess nobody wanted to wait and see if he would. The village threw Ben out, and he lived for a while by raiding the houses on the edge of town, stealing food and stuff. Mr. Keats figured out that the folks were leaving plates of food and blankets out on purpose, where they knew Ben could steal them. So Mr. Keats went into the Meetinghouse one morning and preached and hollered that anyone being nice to Benjamin was a friend of the devil and would pay with an eternity of suffering.

What Mr. Keats didn't get was that the people in town weren't doing it to be nice. They did it because they were scared. They thought it was better to give Ben what he wanted than to have him sneak into their homes. After Mr. Keats yelled at them, they banded together to take care of Ben once and for all. It was against the puritanical spirit of things, so Mr. Keats pretended he didn't know about it even though he overheard Alex's dad talking about it.

It was like a scene out of Frankenstein, all these colonial guys grabbing pitchforks and torches and searching the woods for Benjamin, who ran deeper and deeper into the woods. They finally let him go, but he was so deep in the wilderness, he was completely lost and really alone and scared.

```
         The    wilderness    abounds    with
    monsters  that  take  many  forms,  some
    never   imagined  · by   storytellers.
    The  monster  discovered  by  Benjamin
    was  neither  beast  nor  fiend,  but  a
    brilliant  cold  blue  fire,  as  alive  as
    the woods themselves.
```

That was the fungal wrath.

Benjamin realized the power of the fungus and moved some of the spores to Keatston, casting them along the ground so they could take root. The townspeople were scared of the mushrooms as soon as they saw them, taking them to be an evil omen or some kind of witchcraft. They tried to destroy them, but the mushrooms kept creeping back in the night. Bailey described the various clumps of fungus fusing together underground, making one enormous monster that got bigger and bigger until it was ready to swallow up the village.

William Keats gathered all the people into the Meetinghouse and swore them protection; they huddled and waited for the fungal wrath to consume them. The ground quaked. . . .

And that was the last page I had. The manuscript—or at least what I had of it—ended there.

Dad called us down to dinner. Mom wasn't there, so I guessed that she was busy trying to track down Mandy again. We could hear cars cruising up and down the street. People still wanted to ooh and aah at the glowing mushrooms, but not as many people were parking and running out into the woods. They didn't need to. The mushrooms were plentiful right along the street.

"Did you get some rest?" Dad asked.

"Sure," I said. "I can probably go back to school tomorrow."

"Oh, school is canceled," he said.

"Really?" I asked. Brian also looked up in surprise.

"We got a call. Some parents have complained about the mushrooms. They think they might be toxic."

"Cool," said Brian. "Will they turn us into monsters?"

"No, they'll just make you sick," said Dad.

"Only if you eat them," I said. "Or if you're allergic." I remembered Allan's wheezing. It was probably his parents who complained. I'd have to send them a thank-you card.

"I was only kidding," said Brian.

"The school board wants the mushrooms tested to make sure they're safe," Dad said. "There may not be an immediate effect, but over time . . . who knows?"

I imagined scientists in coats taking slices of mushroom, dropping chemicals on them with eyedroppers, and putting them under a microscope.

"What if they are toxic?" I asked. "They're in our house."

"Then we'll all move to Boston for a while. It'll be like a vacation."

"What about Mom's job?" asked Brian.

"Everything will be fine," Dad said, dodging the question.

Mom came home, and I heard her and Dad arguing from up in my room. I couldn't tell what it was about, but I did hear Dad finally shout out: "You know what, I don't blame her! If I was stuck at that school, I'd run away too!"

"You mean like you ran away from home?" Mom snapped.

The front door opened and shut, but I didn't know which one of them was storming out until I heard Mom's footsteps on the stairs. I heard her talking to Brian, telling him things were all right, then going to her own bedroom. She didn't stop and talk to me, but my lights were off. Maybe she figured I'd slept right through the fight. Maybe she thought I was man enough to handle it.

When it got quiet, I went down the stairs in the dark, the mushrooms lighting my path like the runway lights at an airport guiding in an airplane. I'd never actually been on an airplane, but I'd seen scenes like that in movies. The steps seemed creakier than usual. The mushrooms had grown back in the family room but seemed feeble. The light was a sickly yellowish green instead of the usual bluish green. Dad's battles were helping a little. I sat down in the toxic light and thought some more about Ben Keats. I needed to go back to Howard's and find the rest of the manuscript. The answer had to be in there how Keats saved the Keatston Meetinghouse from getting smashed to smithereens like everything else in town. That was assuming any of it was real, which was a lot to assume. I knew parts of it were real: William Keats founded a town called Keatston, and something happened to it.

Maybe I could go to the museum and talk to one of the old folks who lecture kids when they come on school trips. The problem was that the museum wouldn't even be open again until after Halloween, and for that matter I was probably banned for life.

I was turning into Mandy, I thought, reading and researching instead of taking action. I didn't need to be digging in the past; I needed to be digging in the *soil*. I'd read about it on Wikipedia, that the fungus was one big organism with a heartlike center. I knew where the center was, too—

right in the middle of that black circle in the woods, where we saw the mushrooms for the first time. That was where the fungus started growing, so the core had to be there. Why not dig it up? All I needed to do was find the core and put a stake through it, or crush it with a big stone. You did that with vampires and werewolves and all kinds of monsters. You stabbed them in the heart.

I went out to see the black circle in the woods as soon as the sun came up. The air was damp and cool, but not cold enough for a frost. The mushrooms were still booming. I walked out on the pile of fallen trees and dead boughs, the wood crunching under my feet. I had to take my hands out of my jacket pockets to steady myself as I clambered up a tree trunk, finding the highest point to survey the area. The spot in the forest was about sixty feet across, maybe wider. The layer of branches was between two and three feet high in places.

I'd imagined picking up a few branches and digging, but this was going to be way more work than I could do by myself. It was more than I could do even if I got Mandy and Brian to help. We needed a lot of people, preferably people with muscles.

I started by calling the one guy who couldn't help at all. "Hey, Randy. It's Eric."

"Dude, it's like five a.m. On a day we don't have school."

"It's eight." I'd waited until it was reasonable to be calling people.

"Well, it's early. What's up?"

I told him about the mushrooms, and my theory of how

we could get rid of them. He was the only one who might halfway take me seriously. He did, too—exactly halfway.

"The news said they'll go away after the first frost," he said.

"What if they don't? Or what if something bad happens first?"

"Like in a Max Bailey story?"

"Exactly like in a Max Bailey story."

He didn't answer for a minute, and I expected him to hang up on me.

"We got to play it like it's all about the trees," he said. "If we tell people there's a fungus getting ready to eat the town, they'll send us both to a shrink."

"Will they care if it's about the trees?"

"They will if I tell 'em they do," he said.

Tom was the first person to show up, walking around the house and meeting me in the backyard. By that time Brian was up, wanting to help. We were piling tools into a wheelbarrow: shovels and spades, axes and saws—anything that might help.

"Hey, guys," he said, really normal, like we hadn't shoved each other around the last time we talked. "I'm here to help."

"Hey," I said back. I hadn't called him, but Randy must have. "Good to see you."

"So you're sure this will make a difference?"

"No, but we have to try something," I said. "Nobody else is doing anything."

"Everything's already infected," he pointed out.

"We have to start somewhere."

"Yeah, I guess so. At least nobody at school will talk about us losing the game."

"I missed school on Friday," I reminded him. "Was everybody talking about it?"

"Not really. They mostly talked about the mushrooms. And they talked about how you ran smack into that goalpost. They would have talked about us winning, if we'd won."

The tools were loaded up, so we threw a football around while we waited. I hadn't realized that Brian was a good receiver. Tom and I took turns tossing him long bombs, and he got right under them. I was beginning to worry nobody else would come when Will's mom dropped him off. A few minutes later three eighth graders walked up the road, wearing their letter jackets and work gloves.

"Is this everybody?" one of them asked.

"So far."

"Who's, like, in charge?"

"Nobody," I said. "All of us."

"All right. Just asking."

I was satisfied. Six guys made a good work crew—seven, with Brian—and we were big for our age. But we ended up with twice that many before we trooped into the woods, and then more guys came, including a few high school kids who'd been Owls last year.

I lost track of exactly who was there, because I was too busy lifting and hauling, axing and sawing—we'd brought almost every tool in the shed out with us. We needed a big area to dump the dead wood, and the only thing I could think of was our own yard. The guys formed an assembly line to cart it off and dump it on the fringe of tall grass between the woods and our house. The wood was crinkly and gave off a cloud of dust when you dropped it.

Brian worked there, breaking up the wood and forming it into a tidy pile. Allan tried to help but didn't last long, even wearing a dust mask. The air made him cough and wheeze too much. Brian had to beg him to leave.

"Eric!" I heard Dad hollering my name, turned around, and saw him at the back door. I went over so we didn't have to shout. Hopefully he wasn't mad about dumping the wood in the yard.

"The football team has an ecology project," I told him. "We're clearing out some of the dead stuff in the woods."

"Sounds awesome," he said. "What are you going to do, plant new trees?"

"Yeah, but not until spring."

"Hm." He scratched his head. "You should be taking it easy, though."

"I actually feel pretty good," I told him. "And the woods are in bad shape. Nobody's doing anything about it. We wanted to do something."

"I know, I know. How about if I go to Papa's and get pizzas for everyone?"

"That would be terrific."

"Sodas too," he said. "And those big chocolate chip cookies they make there."

"Yeah. That would be awesome."

"This is good stuff, Eric," he said. "I'm proud of you."

Chapter 22 THE ABANDONED CABIN

School was canceled again on Wednesday—the county health department had taken the samples, but not all the tests were done. It was a good thing, because even with a dozen guys, it took us well into the second day before we were finished. I'd never worked that hard, not even for football. I was achy all over.

We did more than we needed to. I mean, I would have been happy just dragging enough of the dead trees out of the way to get a shovel into the dirt. But since we'd explained that we were going to ready the ground for new trees, we were committed to clearing out the whole area, and that took some doing.

As soon as everybody left, I grabbed a shovel and a spade from the shed and headed back. I had another two hours of daylight, and that was all I needed. I'd find the core and smash it.

"Whatcha doin'?"

I wheeled around and saw Brian and Allan tagging along.

"Going to kill the fungus, I hope."

"Kill it how?" Brian asked.

"I'm going to rip out its heart," I said.

"Mushrooms don't have hearts," said Allan.

"Funguses do. They have cores."

We reached the big rock at the front of the clearing. I walked to what I thought was the dead center of the clearing, then looked around and decided I was off by a few paces. I went to the left and decided I was still wrong.

"I could go get measuring tape," said Brian. "And flashlights."

"Never mind. We don't know it's right smack-dab in the middle anyway." I picked a spot, grabbed the spade with both hands, and drove it down into the soil with all my might.

"Now that's a piledriver," I said, but the spade had barely made a dent. The forest floor was hard and stony.

"You have to dig harder," said Brian. He was helpful that way.

"Maybe get a jackhammer," said Allan.

"We don't have a jackhammer."

I dropped the spade and grabbed the shovel. I set my foot on the back edge of the blade and put all my weight on it. The blade went in an inch, maybe an inch and a half. I scooped out about a handful of dirt and tried again with the same result. Brian swung the spade at the ground, but it just bounced off.

"Don't whap yourself in the face," I told him as he took another swing and nearly did just that.

"This is dumb," said Allan. "You need a big Caterpillar machine that can rip up the ground."

"Even if we had one, just getting it out here would do

too much damage." I set the shovel aside and knelt, scraping soil away with my hand until I saw the problem. There were tough, stringy cords running just below the surface, spreading out in every direction, forming a network that made it nearly impossible to get into the ground. It would take me hours to dig down, working all by myself, even if I knew exactly where the core was. I was tired enough without having to muscle my way through a steel spiderweb.

The quiet was interrupted by what sounded like an angry moose headed right for us, groaning and crashing through the bushes. A moment later Mandy appeared on Howard's quad, slamming on the brakes when she saw us and popping a rear wheelie about a foot off the ground.

"I want to try that!" Allan shouted.

"I drove it once," Brian told him.

They reached her before I did, begging for a ride.

"You owe me!" Allan said. "I helped rescue you."

"It's true. He did," said Brian. "But I helped more, so I should drive while he rides."

"Not now," she said. "I need to talk to Eric."

"Why, what's up?"

"Howard knows the manuscript is gone," she said. "She called it 'the big one.'"

"What does that mean?"

"It was, like, his masterpiece, I think."

"Is she mad?"

"It's hard to know with her. I don't think she's happy about it. Did you read it?"

"Yeah. It's got everything we need to know except what

we need to know." I told her in five sentences about the psycho kid Benjamin Keats throwing the spores around so the fungus could overtake the town.

"It doesn't even say how the old Meetinghouse survived, but it doesn't matter," I told her. "We're just using science and force." I told her about the fungal core, and that I intended to rip it out of the ground and smash it to pieces.

"Sounds too easy," said Mandy.

"Actually, it's wicked hard, and we don't even know exactly where to dig."

"Allan was right. We need a Caterpillar to come and rip up the ground." Brian imitated one by making his hand into a claw and making low grumbling noises as he scooped imaginary soil and cast it aside. Allan nodded. They were probably thinking if we did get one, they'd both get to operate it.

Mandy watched him for a moment, then turned to me.

"Maybe this is a dumb idea," she said, "but don't you have access to a pig?"

That's how I added "pig thief" to my rapidly growing list of criminal accomplishments.

We went on foot, leaving the quad where it was in case the motor scared Cassie.

"You guys wait here," I said when we got to the back fence. I hurried past the compost heap toward the sty. The sky was just getting dark, and the mushrooms were beginning to brighten.

Michelle's jeep wasn't in the driveway. I would have asked for permission if she was home, but was glad I had an excuse not to. I opened the gate and grabbed Babe. Cassie grunted a couple of times in surprise but trotted after me, through the field and into the woods. Pigs are faster than you might think, even a big one like Cassie. I wasn't sure how she'd do in the woods, but she didn't have much trouble with the rocky but mushroom-padded path. She didn't even get distracted—she kept her eyes on Babe and followed like a loyal cocker spaniel. Mandy and Brian and Allan trailed after her, shouting encouragement.

"Go, pig, go!" said Allan, clapping his hands. It seemed to do the trick, at least for the first quarter mile.

What Cassie lacked was stamina. We got about one-third of the way there and she started to grumble. About halfway she flopped down and whimpered.

"She's out of shape," I said.

"Aren't we all?" said Mandy.

We weren't far from my house, so I ran in and got the last two chocolate chip cookies from yesterday's lunch, running past Dad in the kitchen.

"What's going on?"

"Cookie emergency," I shouted. I was already halfway down the hall on my way back out the door.

Cassie sniffed at the cookies and got up, followed me for two or three steps, then stopped again. I broke off part of a cookie and let her snatch it out of my hand, then led her a bit farther before giving her another piece.

Fortunately, they were big cookies. We got to the clearing before she finished the first one, and I rewarded her with the second one.

"You should have saved it for the way back," said Mandy.

"Good point, but too late."

"Now what?" asked Allan.

"I don't know," Mandy admitted. "I thought she would find it on her own. Pigs are famous for finding truffles, and truffles are practically the same thing as mushrooms."

"There are mushrooms everywhere, and she doesn't seem to care."

"I know," said Mandy. "It was just an idea. I read this article once that said truffles produce enzymes that girl pigs naturally respond to. The fungus actually wants the truffles to get eaten to reproduce, because the pig drops the spores somewhere else and another fungus grows in the droppings."

"Gross," said Allan.

"It's interesting is all," she said. I kind of agreed with her.

"Maybe if we led her around, she would do something near to the core," I suggested.

"Good idea!" Mandy said.

The problem is pigs aren't dogs. You can't lead them anywhere. I called Cassie, but she just grunted and flopped to her side, looking at me with squinty eyes.

"Find the mushroom core, girl," said Brian. Maybe because she liked Brian or because she was overcome by fungal enzymes or because the sugar from the cookies kicked in or because of all three, Cassie suddenly jumped up and galloped around the clearing. After a couple of laps she snorted and started circling inward on a spiral. We had to jump out of the way to avoid getting upended as she passed by. She skidded to a halt and rolled around in the dirt, then got up and scratched at the soil.

"No way," said Allan. "It worked."

"We don't know that yet, but I guess we'll start digging here." I scratched a big X with a branch. "But let's take Cassie home first." It was nearly dark now, except for the eerie blue-green glow the mushrooms cast over everything.

"Let's go, girl," I said, holding up Babe so Cassie would follow me.

She must have had a few too many of those enzymes, because she snorted and scuffed at the ground with her back hoof like a bull getting ready to charge, then bolted toward me like a bullet.

I braced myself and dug in with my heels. I caught her shoulder with my shoulder, rolled, and tried to make the tackle, but she squirted away, getting me good in the shin with one of her hooves before she sprinted off into the woods.

I took off after her, but she was too quick, disappearing into some bushes in the distance.

"We'll get the quad!" Mandy shouted after me. I waved to let her know I'd heard her but didn't take my eyes off the forest in front of me. I couldn't see any movement anymore, and couldn't even hear rustling. I followed broken twigs and flattened ferns amid the glare of mushrooms. Cassie couldn't have gone far. She was already tuckered out from her walk out here.

The darkness fell fast, and soon I was lost in the bright sea of mushrooms. I trekked on, zigging and zagging between the trees, listening for Cassie's snorts and breaths. I was way off the path and didn't care. I couldn't go home without Cassie anyway.

I'd expected to hear the roar of the quad, but they must have lost track of me as quickly as I lost track of Cassie.

An hour later I started to wonder if I'd made a big mistake trying to find a lost pig in the dark woods, and two hours later I knew I had. All around me there was nothing but dark forest speckled with blue-green fungus. Nothing looked familiar. I'd heard that you're supposed to stay put when you're lost in the woods. That way if they send out a search party, you won't keep missing each other. It made perfect sense but was hard to live by. I couldn't just pull up a bed of mushrooms and wait until morning. I blundered on through the woods, even though I was so tired I could barely keep putting one foot in front of the other.

I found an ancient narrow trail and decided to stick to it. It had to go somewhere, and anywhere was better than lost. Then the trail petered out in the trees. All right, some trails did that. I'd turn around and walk the other way. There was no such thing as a trail that petered out at both ends.

But wait—there was a square of something gray against the blue-green light. I blinked, seeing rust-colored dots swim in front of my tired eyes. Yes, there was something there. Something rectangular. I stepped closer and nearly cracked my head on the wall of a cabin.

I reached out to touch cool stone walls. It must be old.

Nobody made stone buildings anymore. I followed the stones around the building in search of a door.

It was a strange little building with no windows. Maybe somebody had lived there year-round and built it that way to keep it warmer in the winter. I finally found the door on my second time around. There was no handle. I reached into the crack between the door and the jamb to pull the door open. It was wedged tight, and I practically ripped my fingernails off prying it open. When I did, a wave of stale air wafted out, smelling like grave dirt and rotten eggs.

Inside was absolute blackness, and this time I didn't even have a phone or a pumpkin light. I went back outside and yanked some mushroom caps off their stems. It took more than a little tug to do it; those things were tough.

They made a poor lantern, and when I cast it around inside, I saw strange shadows of sinister objects, angles and blades and saw teeth. Hunting and trapping gear, I guessed. There might have been a lantern and oil among the ancient gear, but I wasn't going to grope around wildly. I didn't want to grab the wrong end of a knife or put my hand in a rusty trap. I felt like a step in any direction would lead to my doom.

I turned around and couldn't find the door. I waved the glob of blue-green light in front of myself, feeling my way along the wall, and banged my head on a board, which clattered to the ground. I'd upended a shelf. I took a step and booted something, heard it ricochet off the wall, and felt it come back to whap me in the shin. It was surprisingly painful. I swore and hopped around for a minute, then stooped over and felt carefully on the earthen floor to check what it was. I found an oddly shaped lump of hard wood.

I heard the roar of a motor through the stone walls and what might have been a voice calling my name. I crammed the mystery thing into my pocket and forgot about the jagged and sharp things that were everywhere, feeling around madly in the dark until I found the door and kicked it open.

"I'm here!" I bellowed. "I'm here!"

The roar was fading, but I ran after it.

"Here! I'm here!" I shouted, waving my arms.

The roar stopped, then started up again, getting louder. I jumped up and down until I saw the headlight. I'd never been happier to see anything.

The quad sputtered to a stop, and Mandy and Brian came on foot across a patch of woods the quad couldn't take, each of them waving a flashlight. Allan must have gone home.

"What is this place?" Mandy waved her flashlight beam at the stone building.

"Nothing, just an abandoned cabin. Did you find Cassie?"

"She went straight home," she said. "We went to get the quad and she was already there."

"She must have circled around," I said. I was so relieved, I laughed. "That pig can take care of herself!"

"Pigs have excellent homing instincts," Mandy agreed.

"You know a lot about pigs."

"Well, maybe I looked them up after I got to know one," she admitted.

"That's cool."

"Michelle was home when we got there," said Brian. "She knows."

"Oh, great." I was never going to get my job back, but at least Cassie was safe and at home. Which was more than I could say for us.

Chapter 23 THE HEAVIER HAMMER

I thought it would be way past midnight when Brian and I finally straggled in, but I saw by the clock on the cable box that it was barely ten.

"There you guys are," said Dad. He was on the couch, tuning his guitar. The house reeked of the fungicide stuff he was spreading everywhere, but I was starting to like that smell. It smelled like victory. "Did you go have dinner with some of the other kids? You should have told us."

"Uh, no, we were still doing stuff in the woods," I said.

"Don't forget you have school tomorrow," said Dad.

"Seriously?" For some reason I'd assumed we wouldn't have to go back until the mushroom nightmare was over.

"The tests said they were safe to be around unless you have allergies."

"Great." It didn't seem fair to let some kids out of school and not everyone.

"Don't complain. If you miss too many days, they'll have to make the school year longer." He stopped, flipped the guitar over, and brushed at the back. "I'm lucky the fungus didn't get at my baby here. Got a big gig lined up."

"What? Really?"

"Is it in Boston?" Brian asked.

"No, it's right here. They're putting together a thing." He strummed his guitar and seemed to like the way it sounded. "They're calling it the Foxfire Festival. People have been coming up to see the mushrooms, so why not make some money? I made some calls and said Arkham Hat Shop could headline. So we're on for Friday."

"What if the mushrooms die before then?"

"That would be bad for the Foxfire Festival," he admitted.

When I emptied my pockets to get undressed for bed, I found the thing that had whacked me in the leg. It was a carving of a little man, similar to the one that Brian found and I broke. This one had a broad hat, his hand raised up high, and his mouth open. He looked like a preacher. In fact, he looked exactly like the kind of preacher who'd go on and on about devil's fire, the wrath of God, and the seeds of redemption being in the people.

A head injury is a great way to get back in good with people. I don't mean you should bang your head on a post in front of the whole school if you're not popular, but it helps.

"Hey, great game," everyone said, and "How are you doing? How's your head?"

"Better," I said. "Thanks for asking."

Most of the day went normally, but we had another all-school assembly at the end of the day.

First the principal welcomed everybody back to school.

He said that the mushrooms weren't a big deal and we should feel safe, and launched into a talk about fund-raising. We were also going to sell Foxfire Festival commemorative buttons, and he said kids who could draw mushrooms and/or operate a Badge-a-Minit could skip one class on Friday to help out.

"That's wonderful," Ms. Brookings said after she grabbed the mike from him. "And now I'd like to say a FEW WORDS."

She started off by saying, "The Foxfire Festival sounds like GREAT FUN and a chance to show your school SPIRIT." Something told me her heart wasn't in it. "I'm not familiar with the music of AKRON HAT STORE," she said, "but it will be SO MUCH FUN."

She segued into a different topic.

"You know, while I'm up here, I really want to thank our football team, who showed some real HEROISM. I don't mean by winning a championship, because they DIDN'T." Thanks for reminding us, I thought. "They did play a very good game and we should APPLAUD them." She patted one palm with her fingers, and there was a smattering of applause from the bleachers. "But one of the boys on that team, you know, had a bad injury, but he still saw a GOOD CAUSE and showed LEADERSHIP in getting his peers to help clean up the woods, so please give him a big ovation. Thank you, RANDY WEAVER."

Everyone clapped and turned to look at Randy. I clapped right along with them. It was my idea, but he really was the one who made it happen. Besides, he loves that kind of attention, and I don't.

। । ।

I didn't even go into the house when I got home. I went straight for the shed, grabbing a shovel and a heavy-duty rake. I was going to dig up the fungal core before I did anything else.

"Where are you going?" Mom called from the back door.

"I got stuff to do."

"It seems like you're never home anymore, especially when *I'm* home. Why don't you come inside?"

"But . . ." I was going to save the town from a mushroom monster. Didn't she understand that?

"I have your shoes," she said. "Pumas?"

"Oh." I'd last seen those shoes in the library at Alden. Somebody had turned them over to Mom, and she knew that they were mine. She paid more attention than I thought. I came inside and found the Pumas sitting there in the family room, with bright white new laces sticking out against the black canvas. They were supposed to have black laces.

Brian was on the couch, putting on his own old shoes and new laces. He looked up just long enough for me to tell that he was as confused as I was.

"You should take better care of your things," Mom said. "Oh, wait . . . I also have something for Brian." She dug through her purse and came up with a library card. "You're not supposed to lend it to anyone," she told him, tossing it on the coffee table.

"I won't anymore," he said. He must have given it to Mandy so she could use the computers, maybe the first time he met her. I was beginning to think he knew her better than I did.

"Do whatever you want until dinnertime, but don't wander off. We're going to have dinner at the table like a family. We have something important to talk about."

Brian looked at me and mouthed, "What's going on?" I shook my head.

"Your father's picking up Firelight," said Mom.

Firelight was my favorite restaurant. Barbecue pork ribs that fall off the bone, only—

"He's getting the rotisserie chicken," Mom said.

"Sounds good."

Dad not only got the chicken and all the sides, but brought enough for a family of eight. I took three pieces and a huge scoop of mashed potatoes, two corn muffins, and a forkful of coleslaw for show.

"This is great, thanks." I ladled gravy over the potatoes.

Mom and Dad nibbled at their own food, but Brian was hungry for once, eating two pieces of chicken, skin and all, and lots of potatoes and slaw. I had the uncomfortable feeling that they were warming us up for some bad news, but I ate anyway. I couldn't think of any news that would make me less hungry.

"There's apple pie, too, so save space," Mom said.

Firelight sells pies, but usually, even the rare times that Mom or Dad got takeout from Firelight, they didn't get the pie. It was especially weird because Mom had found our shoes and probably knew we'd helped Mandy. Maybe this was our last meal? I hoped Mom would wait until after the pie to tell us what our means of execution would be.

"Your father and I have been talking," Mom said. So she wasn't going to wait. The lump of food in my stomach turned into cement as I waited for the verdict.

"Well, we decided it's time to call it quits," she said.

I traded looks with Brian. Suddenly Mom's casual attitude about us breaking and entering at Alden made a little bit of sense. She didn't want to bring the hammer down when she knew a bigger, heavier hammer was about to come down on both of our heads.

"You mean you're getting divorced?" I asked.

"Yes," she said. "No more living apart but still being married. No more living together and feeling like we live apart anyway." She was doing all the talking. Dad was looking off into the distance.

"Okay," I said. Dad would move back to Boston and try to be a rock star, and I'd go on with my life. I had a fungus to kill, and I would have to go to court for the incident at the museum, but eventually things would go back to normal—or as normal as they were a few weeks ago, which was normal enough for me.

Brian was less accepting. He glowered, dropping his fork and crossing his arms. He looked back and forth from Mom to Dad to me, and I knew that he hated all of us.

"That's not all," Dad said. He shoved his plate aside and leaned in, putting his hands on the table and interlocking his fingers. "I want you both to come live with me in Boston.

I'm excited about it, and your mother also thinks it's a good idea. We'll need to have a lot of work done on this house, and it'll be easier if nobody's living here. I mean, nobody but your mother."

I lost all interest in the pie.

The conversation went on for a while. Dad would have to get a bigger apartment, of course, and he'd look into schools.

"I'll try to find an apartment in Jamaica Plain," he said. "Or at least nothing too suburban. Brookline would be okay. We'll find a cool neighborhood close to the action. You'll love it."

"I'll miss you both so much," Mom said. "I can't even tell you how much. But the house really does need major work, and living in the city will be a great opportunity."

"You're going to love it," said Dad. "There's so much to do. Eric, we can go see the Patriots! And the Red Sox!" He went on and on, trying to tell me everything there was to love about Boston.

"We thought it would be a good time for both of you," Mom said. "Eric especially." She meant that I'd been in so much trouble here, I guessed. I couldn't think of any other reason it was a good time for me to move to another state. I'd have to try out for a new team, and compete against guys the coach already knew.

"Can we go to the zoo?" Brian asked. He was acting like it was only a trip to Boston, not like his whole life was changing.

"Of course," said Dad.

"Yay!"

I wanted to get excited about Patriots games and everything else Dad liked about Boston—the music clubs and sushi restaurants—but the truth was that my favorite thing was getting dragged into the woods at the crack of dawn, even if I grumbled about it, because the world was perfect then. I liked dew on the grass and the occasional raccoon, the sun breaking through the trees, the peace and quiet. I didn't want to live somewhere with a bunch of cars whizzing by and people hurrying everywhere. I didn't want to live in an apartment building with a hundred thousand other people. I especially didn't want to live across the street from a neon sign.

Mom had gone off to the kitchen to get the pie. I heard the oven clicking—she'd been warming it up.

"Are you cool?" Dad asked.

"Sure," I said, even though I wasn't cool. I was upset. Also, I felt guilty because I wasn't thinking about people. I wasn't thinking about Mom or my friends, because I figured there'd be people in Boston, too, and Mom wasn't around much anyway. I was upset because I would miss Maine. I didn't think I could live without it.

Mom came out with the pie, and there was a scoop of cinnamon ice cream on every slice. She really was trying to make this easy on us. I ate mine without another word.

Chapter 24 **THE SCREAMING**

I felt like a zombie as I walked from class to class, saving my button-making break for last. A lot of other kids had the same idea, so there was a total mob scene outside the art room. There were way more people than could fit in the room, but nobody volunteered to go back to class.

"You could make a banner" was the art teacher's idea. She gave us a big roll of paper and some colored pencils. We unrolled it in the gymnasium and set about lettering WELCOME TO TANGLEWOOD! and decorating it with mushrooms and other stuff all around the margins. I drew a football guy passing a ball to another football guy, both of them wearing Owls colors.

"Everything is way out of proportion," said Heidi. She was down at the other end, but her voice carried. "The people are the same size as the mushrooms."

"So what?" Monica asked. Heidi didn't have an answer, so she plopped down and started coloring in the first W.

"We're number two!" Tony joked. He was drawing some owls (some regular bird owls) roosting in the second W.

"Hey, those are really good," I said.

"Thanks. Hey, you owe me an apology."

"For losing to the Oxen?"

"No, for making fun of me in science class."

"I made fun of you?" I didn't have any memory of it.

"You laughed at me for asking if those mushrooms would turn red. You said that only happened in video games. Well, now they are turning red. They're getting ripe."

"Come on."

"Go see for yourself. Check out the football field." He went on drawing his owls.

I put my colored pencil down and went to see. Nobody was keeping track of who was really there anyway. I went out through the locker rooms and saw what he meant.

Over by the home team's bench, the field had gone from blue-green to a flaming orangey red. The cones were even pointier, and when they rustled in the breeze, they looked like fire.

Whether or not they were going to blow up or turn into monsters, Tony was right—they seemed to be ripening.

Brian was so excited for the show, he wanted to leave as soon as we both got home from school.

"It doesn't start until seven," I told him. "It's not even four o'clock yet." I was going to dig up the core and be done with it, and I didn't care about ruining the Foxfire Festival. It was a race against time.

"I want to get a good place," he said. "Come on!" He was jumping up and down. He'd never seen Dad perform before, at least not in front of an audience. Actually, neither had I.

"You really want to stand around for three hours before the show even starts?"

"Yes! Come on!"

We picked up Allan and took our bikes and headed to the park downtown, locking them up behind the pizza place. It didn't look like any of the mushrooms at the park had turned red like the ones at the school. Maybe it would take a few days for the fungus to finish getting ripe, or whatever it was doing.

There were already a lot of people standing around waiting for the show, but we were able to weave our way to the front. About half of them were in costumes, because tomorrow was Halloween—there were a lot of mushroom hats, made out of papier-mâché or green stocking caps stuffed with newspaper. There were also a lot of zombies and hoboes. A few glared at us as we cut in front of them. I'd never been to a rock concert before, but my feeling was that when there were no seats, it was every man for himself.

I saw the school booths off to the side—a couple of eighth-grade girls were selling buttons and baked goods, and the Friends of Keatston were right next to them, pointing people to the haunted house a few blocks away. Papa's had a booth set up, too, and the line didn't look too bad. Most people don't eat dinner at four-thirty in the afternoon.

"Hey, do you guys want food?" I asked them.

"Yeah, I think I want a hot dog," said Allan.

"Bri, I can bring you a slice of pizza if you hold our spot."

"Extra cheese," he said. "And a root beer."

"Got it. Hold our place."

Brian widened his stance, trying to take up as much room as possible.

"Atta boy."

By the time Allan and I made our way back, it was getting packed up front. We had to go around a crowd of college kids who wouldn't let us through. Two of them were wearing Bowdoin sweatshirts, which meant they'd come a long way for our small-town party.

We ate our pizza and drank our soda while the park filled up with people. Way more people than I expected, a lot of them from out of town. I hoped that meant the town was making money.

Some guy came out and thanked everyone for coming, reminded them of all the stuff they should spend money on while they were there, and left the stage. There was another half-hour wait while the sky darkened and the crowd got impatient. Finally the PA system blasted some static, and then a voice rang out.

"Please welcome—all the way from Boston—the Bright Fun Guys!"

Who?

Brian looked at me, his eyes wide in confusion. I patted his shoulder to let him know it was okay. This was an opening band, not a replacement band.

But it was Arkham Hat Shop. Rick came out first, sat down, and started pounding on the bass and tapping on the toms. Then Wade came out and thumped out a familiar bass line. The song was "Relationship," their best-known song. I was surprised they didn't save it for last, but maybe they wanted to hook the crowd with a song we all knew. The audience started clapping along with the drums.

Dad got the biggest round of applause, since he was a local. He was a silhouette against the lights, windmilling his arm at the guitar, and I had to admit it was pretty awesome to be his kid right then and there with everyone cheering. Brian was jumping up and down, practically as high as the stage.

Finally the singer came out—Danny—and grabbed the mike.

"We thought we'd try a new name out tonight," he growled, and then a big sign unfurled behind them, reading THE BRIGHT FUN GUYS. The crowd cheered. There's nothing like a bad pun to kick things off.

They ripped through "Relationship" and a few other songs, never taking more than a few seconds between songs. The sound saturated the crowd, the bass and drums sending little shock waves through our feet. It was really high energy, like football, only with more shoving. No wonder Dad loved it so much.

Danny walked off after a few shout-outs to the crowd, and the rest of the band settled into a long instrumental called "Mountain Madness." As the song wound down, the drummer and bass player also left, leaving Dad all alone on the stage. He edged up to the mike, dripping sweat like he'd run a marathon.

"I'm going to do something dumb," he said. The PA system squawked because he was too close to the mike. "I'm going to do something dumb," he repeated.

Please don't be that dumb, I thought.

"This is for my best buddies," he said. He fiddled with a couple of strings on his guitar, then went back and kicked a pedal to soften the sound. He started strumming, a little picking here and there, and I knew the song instantly.

"'Through the woodland, through the valley, comes a horseman wild and free. . . .'"

The crowd seemed to like it okay, but a lot went off to get drinks or hit the porta-potties. They were talking more, too. But it was all right, because Dad wasn't playing it for them. He was playing it for Brian and me. I was kind of touched and teary-eyed.

He carried on through the song, asking who the brave young horseman could be. When he was done, he muttered that the band would be right back, set the guitar on its stand, and disappeared. There was still some humming noise, and a sound guy ran to make sure the amps were muted and the mike was off.

"I need to go," Brian said. I thought he wanted to say hi to Dad, but then I saw his one-leg-then-the-other dance. He meant "go" as in "to the bathroom."

"All right, let's go."

We got at the end of the porta-potty line, which was pretty long. I passed the time looking for friends, but it was hard to see anyone because of all the people.

"I didn't think this many people lived in the whole county!" Allan said.

"They don't," said Brian. "They're from all over."

"Oh, yeah."

Did Mom come? I wondered. She should have come, but it didn't seem likely.

"Boo!"

Somebody nudged me from behind. I wheeled around and saw Mandy wrapped up in a scarf, with a wool hunting cap perched on her head.

"You look like Elmer Fudd," I said.

"What's up, Doc?" she asked in a bad Bugs Bunny voice.

"Wrong character!" Brian said.

"Whatever, Doc."

Brian's turn finally came to use the toilet, and he ran off to do so.

"You decided to check out the festival?" I asked Mandy. It surprised me that she'd take the chance of getting busted.

"I heard that Arkham Hat Shop was playing," she said.

"You've heard of them?"

"Yes! I've got a lot of their songs. They're cool. The singer is awesome."

"Yeah. Brian likes them a lot."

Another porta-potty door opened and Allan took off for it. There were only four. The line behind us had gotten long.

"He's *heard* of Arkham Hat Shop?" said Mandy. "He's cooler than I thought. So you're not a fan?"

"They're all right."

"It's cool to see them live," she said. "I didn't think they were together anymore. They're old, too. The guitar player used to be really hot."

My turn came at the portable toilet.

"Excuse me," I told Mandy. "I have to throw up."

I didn't really, but I did have to go. When I got out, the band was back on the stage. Everyone packed the stage, and I couldn't see Brian or Allan or Mandy anywhere.

Danny came up to the microphone.

"I'm going to have the guys bring these lights down . . . ," he said. The spotlight dimmed, and he kept gesturing to go down more until all the lights around the band were off and we could see the mushrooms flaring up behind them. The crowd was quiet but started cheering when they realized what he was doing. The band launched into a song called "I'm Beginning to See the Light."

The crowd loved it, punching the air and hooting and swaying to the music. My dad had a long solo, and the singer came back for another verse and another chorus. They finished with a huge crescendo and a round of applause that went on and on, a lot longer than I expected. Then I realized that the band wasn't playing and that most of the crowd had fallen quiet, but there was still a loud screechy noise in the air, coming from everywhere.

The mushrooms were *screaming*.

Chapter 25 THE HEART OF THE MONSTER

The caps were turning inside out like umbrellas on a windy day. They seemed to be moving—not rustling in the wind, but wriggling and struggling to break free of the ground. And all of them were making a racket, none of them in quite the same key. It was a total cacophony.

All at once everybody was running every which way across the park. I realized that people might get trampled and moved back toward the porta-potties, still looking for Brian. I called his name, but it was impossible to be heard over the racket. I thought I saw him running in the distance and took off after him, but I only got about twenty yards before I was knocked flat by a big guy running the other way. Feet thundered by my ears, and I was sure I would get stepped on. I got to my knees and stopped.

There was a mushroom not far from me—a really broad cap, turned inside out so I could see the gills vibrating. That was how they made noise—they were like a billion string instruments, their caps made into megaphones. They were able to reach Metallica-like volume because there were so many of them.

Somebody grabbed me and pulled me up.

It was Mandy. I watched her mouth opening and closing, her arms gesturing, and shook my head. I couldn't hear a thing.

"I have to find Brian!" I shouted back. She shook her head and cupped her ear.

It was impossible to hear anything.

"Come on!" she shouted. I could read her lips.

She ran, and I followed a herd of people heading down Keatston Street. A lot of people were getting into their cars, but once their cars were started, there was nowhere to go— the street was clogged with people and other cars. I saw one guy pounding on his horn, but nobody could hear him, so he opened the door and started yelling, and we couldn't hear that either.

There were Brian and Allan, stopped in the middle of the road, looking around. I waved, but Brian didn't see me until I actually nabbed him.

"Bikes!" I shouted.

"What?" I saw his lips open and guessed the word. I mimed like I was grabbing handlebars and he nodded. We ran around behind the restaurant. It was just as noisy, but there were no people and it felt calmer. I pointed out the bikes and Mandy nodded.

We slalomed through the crowd, Allan on his bike, Mandy on Brian's, and Brian parked on the seat behind me. It was slow going until we broke free of the crowd; then we were able to pedal like mad until we turned off on our own street. Allan veered off into his driveway. His parents were waiting for him on the porch.

I sped on right into our backyard and used my feet to help brake the bike. Brian jumped off.

"We're going to kill this thing!" I shouted. "You go inside."

"No!" He shook his head. I shoved him toward the back door. I didn't have time to argue. He sulked but went in.

Mandy caught up with me.

"Did you take the quad out here?" I shouted.

"Yeah, but it's way over there!" she shouted back, gesturing to a little-used side trail. "I didn't want anyone to find it!"

We didn't have to shout. The mushrooms had fallen silent, but it took us a moment to realize because our ears were still ringing.

"Never mind," I said. "It's not that far."

"What do you want to do?" Mandy asked.

"We're going to kill it," I told her.

I grabbed a flashlight and a bunch of tools from the shed, and we set out through the forest to the clearing. I felt jangly and jittery, like I did before football games. I took the shovel and an ax, and Mandy carried a flashlight and a saw.

We shone the light around the clearing, searching for the spot Cassie had marked, and found my nearly invisible X in the dirt. I grabbed a shovel and brought it down with all my might, barely getting it into the tough dirt and immediately hitting a gnarly mass of fungus. I scraped away the soil, exposing the neon cords—the roots lit up at night, too. Mandy went to work with the ax while I moved over and kept digging.

We worked like that for a long time, trading tools a few times, barely talking because our ears were still numb from the noise at the park. We slowly unearthed an enormous knot of brightly lit cords and began chopping and sawing at it and taking it apart.

It was nearly dawn when we felt a tremor in the ground. We'd cleared a hole about three feet around and three feet deep and were still working at the cords. The tremor was slight, like you feel when someone drops something heavy on the floor.

The fungus was moving beneath us.

I tried to pick up the pace even more, but my body felt like it was made of jelly. Sweat and dirt filled my eyes, and all I could do was try to wipe my face with my shirt, which was filthy from the work.

There was a roar in the distance, and a moment later Brian appeared on the quad.

"I brought food and water," he said. "I made peanut butter sandwiches, and I brought the first aid kit in case anybody got hurt. Oh, and I brought Dad's camping kit!"

"Brian," said Mandy, "you're a hero." She took a bottle of water and guzzled it.

"Thanks, man." I went for the water first, drinking half a bottle and using the rest to wash my face a little. I used a ratty towel from Dad's camp bag to dry off.

"We really appreciate it, but maybe you better go back?" I suggested.

"But I want to help!" said Brian.

"I don't know if it's safe."

"Then you shouldn't be here either."

He had a point.

"Somebody has to do something," I said.

"Hey, three people would be better than two," Mandy whispered to me.

"Fine." I couldn't win an argument with her on his side. "All right, but stay out of the hole. We need someone to help us out later anyway."

"Okay," said Brian.

Mandy and I went back into the hole to work with new energy, scooping out more dirt and sawing apart the fungal branches. They got thicker and thicker as we went deeper. Brian paced the edge of the hole, asking us every few minutes if we needed anything.

The hole was now almost five feet deep. It might not be easy to get out again, but we kept digging. I pulled on a particularly stubborn cord and saw something tucked under it, off to the side.

"Look." I pointed it out to Mandy—it looked like there was a ball in there, shining as brightly as a streetlight bulb.

"Is that the heart?" she asked.

"It must be."

I dropped to my knees and went to work with an ax, hacking at cords as thick and fleshy as young trees. They splintered and slivered but refused to break. Mandy worked the other side with a saw, so we were on the same wavelength—if we could lift out this chunk of fungal root, we could get at the heart thing below it.

I've come to doubt my memory of what happened next. I mean, I do remember it, but when I play it out, none of it seems believable.

First there was another tremor, and I heard a deep grinding noise, like a tectonic plate sliding deep in the earth. I could see Mandy's mouth open and close without a sound, while Brian shouted from somewhere behind me. The ground shook beneath us, and loose soil started to dance around the edge of the hole. I stumbled and dropped the ax. The blunt side glanced off my knee and sent a spasm of pain radiating up my body.

I saw Mandy stumble too, the ground quaking beneath her. The cord we'd been hacking at lashed out like a tentacle, whipping over my head and slapping the edge of the hole. I grabbed the ax, reached over, and gave it a few whacks. It must have come loose, flopping out like a giant spring and making the ground shift under us.

"Come on!" Brian shouted. "Let's go!" He was on the edge of the hole, holding out a hand to help me out. I shook my head no. We were here to fight this thing.

The grinding noise became louder and the ground erupted. Mandy lost the saw in a jumble of cords, kicked at a big fungal tentacle, and turned around, tripping as her foot got caught in a snarl. I pulled her free, striking at the tentacle with the ax even as the fungus rose up from the ground and rained dirt around our heads and shoulders.

I felt a loop come around my waist. I dropped the ax and tried to pry the thing off me, but it picked me up and flipped me upside down like it was going to administer the piledriver, Undertaker-style.

I could see the core beneath me, a ball of pink among the green. It was not as big as I expected—no bigger than a football, actually. There was a gaping wound in it where we'd cut off the major cord, and it was now connected only by some smaller, stringier cords radiating around it. I wondered if I could take it away, like I was forcing a fumble. I needed to free myself for one second.

Something whizzed by, I heard a splintering crunch, and the shovel tumbled past my head, nearly taking my ear with it. Brian must have hurled it like a spear into the cord around my waist. The grasp on me loosened, and I dived toward the heart of the monster. I grabbed the corners with my hands and twisted, letting my falling body weight do the work. There was a series of snaps as the strings holding the core broke. I dug my fingernails into the spongy ball so I wouldn't lose it. I was whapped and walloped by hard-hitting weights piling up on me, but I'd been there before—a dog pile after a fumble—and knew what to do, which was protect the ball. I felt the fingers of the fungus poke and prod at my arms as they tried to work the core free, but I held on tight and waited as they gave a last desperate grab, then twitched and were still.

At least I remember it that way. The more I try to re-create it, exactly as it happened, the more it feels like a vivid nightmare I had long ago.

Mandy pulled the cords off me until a little window of morning light opened above my head. I crawled out, still holding the heart. Brian helped each of us out of the hole, grabbing our hands so we could clamber up the side.

The fungus looked like nothing now—a twisted mess of thick twine and ropes, dead on the ground. In the trees past the clearing, I saw the mushrooms dimming. I still held the core, which was now white and felt as lifeless as a hunk of wood.

"That's all?" said Mandy.

"I guess so."

Brian took it from me and drove the shovel into it, dead center. It split open like a big potato. There was no blood and not so much as a whimper. I'd forgotten it was just a fungus.

"I thought it would be harder," he said.

"Me too." I almost felt sorry for it.

Chapter 26 THE BIGGEST SECRET

We heard voices and saw flashlights slashing through the trees, and a moment later some police came stomping into the clearing. One of them got on the radio and barked into it: "Three seventy-two niner five a zero." I don't remember exactly.

"Let's go," he said to Mandy. She went. There were no handcuffs and no threats.

"What is the nature of this vehicle?" another officer asked me, pointing at the quad.

"Mostly a Royal Enfield quadricycle," I told him, looking around to make sure Brian was okay. He was talking to another cop and pointing back at me.

"It's got a newer motor and some odds and ends from other things," I told the cop.

"Is the vehicle yours?"

"No, but I borrowed it from somebody. Well, she borrowed it." I gestured at the space where Mandy had been standing a few minutes ago. "The owner knows we have it. She's a friend of ours."

"Did you know it's against state law to take motorized vehicles on these paths?"

"No."

"And did you know you have to be a licensed driver at least sixteen years of age to drive a motorized vehicle of any kind?"

"No."

"We'll need to confiscate this vehicle," he said.

"But I've got to return it," I said. "It belongs to this old woman—it's her only means of transportation."

"Son, we'll see that the vehicle is returned to the proper owner." He really liked the word "vehicle."

I gave him Howard's name, but I didn't know her address. "She lives close to the highway," I said, "halfway between here and Boise Township. I don't even know if she has a phone."

He muttered something into the radio and waved me away. I was free to go, but without the quad. Brian was also done being interrogated, and we headed home. The mushrooms crumbled under our feet as we walked through the backyard.

"Kids, you're all right!" Dad said when Brian and I came in. "I didn't have any idea what happened to you. Everything was such a scene . . . all the screaming, and the stampede. It was nuts. Your mother slept in her office at Alden because the radio said not to even try to drive into Tanglewood. I thought maybe you were laying low at a friend's house, but when you didn't call . . ."

"We were killing the fungus," said Brian.

"What?" Dad shook his head in confusion.

"Did you notice the mushrooms are all dead?" I asked him.

"The TV news said it was the frost," he said.

Did it get cold enough for a frost? I was working too hard to notice, but I should have noticed. I would have seen my breath, felt my own sweat get icy on my skin. I didn't remember seeing a coat of white on the lawn when we came home, either.

"It wasn't frost," said Brian.

"I'm just telling you what they said on TV," said Dad.

"They're lying," I said.

"The weatherpeople don't lie," he said. "I mean, not *after* the weather. They have instruments."

"Forget the frost," I said. "What did they say about the screaming mushrooms?"

"Well, it's like, uh . . . some people say that they think they heard the *mushrooms* screaming, but the TV news said—and I think so, too—they said it was feedback from the speakers and that maybe people were wound up a little tight and overreacted."

"I saw the mushrooms scream," I told him. "I mean, I heard them. But I also *saw* them." Brian nodded.

"Yeah, well. You had a bad knock in the head not so long ago," said Dad. "I'm starting to worry about both of you guys."

I said a bad word, right in front of him, and stormed up the stairs, Brian stomping up after me.

Tanglewood was on the national news that night. They showed downtown—store windows that had been shattered and boarded up, broken glass and garbage scattered in the street. "A small town in Maine is recovering from a festival gone awry," the news commentator said grimly. They went to a reporter standing in front of the Keatston Meetinghouse.

"I've heard that the riot occurred during the encore of a band called the Bright Fun Guys, when some deafening feedback from the speakers sent the crowd stampeding down Main Street," the guy said. He didn't say one word about the mushrooms, and he got the name of the street wrong.

The next bit was the mayor, standing in front of the post office, which is the closest thing Tanglewood has to a city hall.

"You have to remember that we hosted an event with people from all over the state," she said, "including a number of college students who might have had a bit more to drink than was advisable. We're a peaceful little town, and I don't believe anyone from Tanglewood was directly responsible for this escalation of events."

Disorderly college kids, that was all they talked about. I could have kicked in the TV.

It was Halloween, but nobody went trick-or-treating that year. It was like the whole town forgot, or simply had had enough of spooky fun. I also forgot about football on Sunday. When I turned on the news later and saw the scores, it was kind of a jolt. Everywhere else around the country, football and life were going on like it was just another week. The Patriots had their bye week anyway, so I didn't miss much.

• • •

We had more of the same at school on Monday. They scheduled a special morning assembly meant to tell us nothing happened.

"Well, I hope you all REMEMBER what can happen if a number of people behave IRRESPONSIBLY," said Ms. Brookings. There was a whole lot of "I told you so" in her voice, even though she hadn't officially told us so.

Somebody up front mumbled something about the mushrooms. Usually she rushed to students who had something to say and gave them the mike, like a daytime talk show host, but this time she shook her head.

"I'm hearing a lot of PREPOSTEROUS and IMPOS-SIBLE explanations for what occurred," she said. "Let's call these what they are: EXCUSES. There's no EXCUSE for the terrible BEHAVIOR we witnessed this weekend."

"What about the screaming mushrooms?" somebody hollered.

"I can't. I can't," the counselor said, shaking her head, like it was the most ridiculous thing she'd ever heard. She handed the microphone to the principal, who muttered that we all had to go back to class.

I started to wonder myself when I was trying to get to sleep that night. What had happened? Was I sure about what I'd seen? Was I even sure about what I'd experienced? I knew we'd been in the woods and dug up the core, and I knew Brian had driven a shovel through it. But had it really fought back? Maybe we were overtired, overworked, and half asleep. Maybe a big hunk of cord sprang out of the ground and looked alive for a second. Maybe I'd gotten knotted up with the cords and imagined the fungus was wrestling with me.

I could ask Brian, but he had an overactive imagination. I might have trusted Mandy's memory a little bit better—a very little bit—but I didn't know how to get ahold of her. I'd spent too much time with both of them—that was the problem.

I found Allan after the assembly. He was back at school since the mushrooms had disappeared.

"You heard the screaming, right?"

"I don't know," he admitted. "It was just, like, an earsplitting noise. It was coming from everywhere."

He was no help at all.

I woke up before dawn sensing that something was wrong. I pushed the curtains aside on my bedroom window. The mushrooms were back, scattering dime-sized dots of blue-green across the yard.

I went outside to get a better look. The stems were half the height they'd been at their largest, but the fungal network had already been in place, ready to poke its million gnome-hatted heads out of the ground.

Either the fungus didn't really need its core or it could simply grow a new one. Either way, we were doomed.

Mr. Davis was on his back porch, looking glum.

"Thought we got rid of these fellas," he said.

"Me too."

"They got into the house, you know. Probably bring it

down. Don't know if my insurance will cover it if they do." He stood up, shook his head, and went inside.

On the other side of our house, Sparky was growling and digging into the yard, scattering a dozen caps. Ms. Fisher peeked from the back door but didn't come outside.

"Come on, punkin," she hollered, but Sparky kept on digging.

I was with Sparky. We needed to fight back. I just didn't know what to do anymore.

"Are the mushrooms going to blow up?" Tony asked in science class.

"Interesting question." Ms. Weller was better than Ms. Brookings about letting us ask questions. "Why do you think they would?"

"Because they're turning red," he said. "The whole field is red now."

I'd forgotten about the red mushrooms. Did they disappear and come back like the green ones? Or did they hold their own?

"I've never heard of mushrooms dramatically changing color," said Ms. Weller. "They might darken when they're done fruiting, but that's one way they *aren't* like apples." She was remembering my own comparison of the fungus to an apple tree, but I didn't think she was trying to make fun of me.

"Well, I never heard of them screaming before, either," I said without raising my hand. There was actually a spattering of soft clapping.

"I'm not convinced we did hear them screaming," the

teacher said. "Now, I admit I wasn't there. But how many of you can really say where a noise comes from, especially a loud one? Have you ever been mistaken, thinking a sound came from inside that was really outside?"

Kids looked around at each other. Sure, that happens sometimes.

"I wonder if anyone has heard of Occam's razor?" She wrote it on the board. Nobody raised their hand. Randy almost did but took it back.

"It's a theory that when you don't know the answer, the simplest explanation is the most likely to be true," she said. "It's not always the right answer, but it's the best guess. For example, if you're missing a quarter and discover there's a hole in your pocket, what do you think happened? Did somebody steal it?"

"No, you probably lost it," Randy answered.

"Exactly," the teacher said. "That's the biggest secret in science. A lot of it isn't about knowing the right answer, just making the best guess."

A few kids snickered.

"Well, the simplest explanation for what happened on Friday night was that some feedback from the speakers spooked the audience and started a stampede. It's *possible* the mushrooms were screaming, but that would mean a whole new species of fungus had come along that had powers beyond any fungus we've ever seen. It's a lot to believe, compared to believing that people simply made a mistake, isn't it? Especially when there was lots of chaos and confusion?"

I raised my hand this time but didn't wait for her to

call on me. "So what is the simplest explanation for the red mushrooms on the football field, if it isn't that some of the mushrooms changed color? Because that seems like the simplest explanation to me."

From across the room Tony held up his hand in a make-believe high five.

"The simplest explanation is that the red ones are a different species of mushroom," the teacher said, extending her hands to me like she was handing me a big ball of obviousness.

If she was right, the red mushrooms were in a real battle for control of the football field, from end zone to end zone, sideline to sideline. The old ones were yellowish white in the daytime, but the red ones were still orangey and bright, their pointed tops looking like tongues of flame, higher and brighter than the yellow ones. The whole field looked like a lake of toasting marshmallows. If people were scared of the green ones, the red ones would really put them into a panic. It would look like a flood of fire pouring into town. That's what the picture in the museum showed, too—red and blue mushrooms mingling, the townspeople screaming and waving their arms.

I felt like there was something there I wasn't seeing. It had something to do with the football field turning red and Max Bailey's story and what my science teacher said about the razor rule. The truth was like the fungus itself, the caps appearing aboveground like separate things, but they were all connected underground and I couldn't see how. I needed to find the dead center of the problem and dig it up, but I didn't know where the center was.

Dad was packing already. Boxing up his books and carrying them up the basement stairs, because this time the move was permanent.

"Just trying to get some of this stuff taken care of now," he said, dropping a box in the hallway.

"Don't forget your Max Bailey book," I told him. "I think it's still in the living room."

"Did you finish it?"

"Nope." I'd actually only read one Max Bailey story, and that one wasn't even in the book.

"Go ahead and finish it. You can pack it with your things. You're coming with me, remember? You might want to get a head start on stuff too, you know." He tousled my hair and went back downstairs.

Oh, yeah. I didn't think we were moving right away. For some reason I thought we'd wait until after the school year, even though nobody said so. But Dad was going to move back to Boston, and Bri and I were going to join him as soon as he found a place.

Allan came down the stairs, looking a little thoughtful. He was wearing a dust mask dangling around his neck.

"What's up?" I asked.

"I'm moving," he said. "I was just saying goodbye to Brian."

"He must be bummed," I said. "I am too." I meant it. "When do you leave?"

"Tomorrow morning. I'm going to spend the rest of the school year in Portland living with my grandma."

"Wow."

"Allergies," he reminded me. "The mushrooms are worse than ever."

"I know. That's a drag. Hey, if you're back this summer, let's play HORSE."

"You're moving too," he reminded me. I'd forgotten for a second, and remembering made me feel a little lurch in my stomach.

I noticed he had the Celtics keychain I'd seen in Brian's drawer.

"Going-away present?"

"It's mine," he said. "I lost it in the trough and Brian kept forgetting to give it back to me."

"The what?"

"I just mean I lost it and Brian found it."

"You lost your keys in the trough? You mean Cassie's trough? How did that happen?"

"It was nothing," he said. He started for the door and turned back. "I'm really sorry about what happened to Cassie, and so is Brian."

"Huh? What happened to Cassie?"

"You know." He hung his head and told me.

238

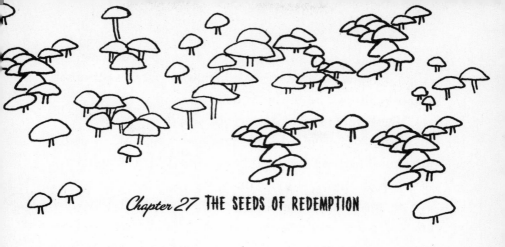

Chapter 27 THE SEEDS OF REDEMPTION

Brian was in his room, watching his hedgehogs nibble at wheat-colored nuggets.

"No bugs?"

"Sometimes they eat hedgehog food," he said.

I watched one of them pick up a pellet with its weird little hands and chisel it down with its pointy teeth. It was kind of cool to watch when it wasn't a bug.

"They remind me of Cassie," I said.

"There's a reason they're called hedge*hogs*," he said.

"Oh, yeah." I waited a bit, not sure how to edge into this topic. "So are you going to miss Allan?"

He shrugged slowly, but there was a lot of sadness in it.

"He just told me you guys were there the night I fought with Randy."

"What?" He looked up at me in what I took to be completely fake astonishment. "He said that?"

"He said you told Tom to do it."

"Allan's a rat fink," he muttered.

"I think you're the rat," I said. "You didn't stand up for

Allan. He said he tried to stop them when Cassie got upset, and they threw him in the trough."

"They were just kidding around. He didn't get hurt."

"Brian . . ." I didn't think he was the kind of kid who'd just stand there while a friend was bullied. "You should have stood up for him," I said again.

"It wasn't like I could stop them," he added. His voice cracked and he started crying. "I told Allan I was sorry. I was scared. They were bigger than me and there were more of them."

I understood that part, but not what led up to it.

"Why would you put yourself into that mess, Bri? You like Cassie."

"I know." He sniffed and reached into the terrarium for one of the hedgies. "You can do something to Digger if you want." He held the hedgehog out to me.

"Brian, that's the last thing I want to do." I laughed at Digger's stunned expression, like she knew she'd been offered up in sacrifice.

"I didn't think it would turn out like that," he said, putting Digger back in the terrarium. "It was supposed to be a joke."

"Not after they dumped Allan in the trough. Not after Cassie started freaking out."

"Okay. Maybe I thought you would start a fight and they would beat you up."

"You wanted guys to beat me up?"

"Not bad. Just a little."

"Brian—" I was about to ask why, but I didn't. I had enough pictures in my head: the make-believe piledriver, pinning him on the bed, shoving him all the time, and ordering him around. I'd put him headfirst into the laundry basket, tossed him on the couch from across the room, and a hundred other things. I'd never actually hurt him, but thinking back on it all made me want to beat myself up a little.

"I'm sorry, buddy."

"You always say that."

"What if I let you punch me right now?" I asked. "You can hit me as hard as you can? Just not in the face or the crotch?"

"Don't be stupid."

"Seriously. I have it coming. You can just haul off and sock me once. I won't fight back. I deserve it."

"I don't want to right now," he said. "Can I wait until the next time I'm really mad at you?"

"Okay," I agreed, but maybe that was a bad idea. I'd seen the steely-eyed way Brian drove that shovel into the fungal core. I'd better not get on his bad side ever again.

We went to see Howard on Saturday. I still had the manuscript, and I was hoping Mandy had left behind a way to contact her. Brian insisted on coming with me. We pedaled out on the highway. The woods were too overtaken with mushrooms.

We knew Howard was home because the quad was parked in the backyard, but we had to bang on the back door for a long time before she answered.

"Oh, it's you two." She opened the door so we could come in. "I thought maybe the police were back. They called me everything from a kidnapper to an accomplice."

"Did you get arrested?" Brian asked. "Eric got arrested a while ago!"

"Bah, I just kept asking if they'd seen Missy Speckle Nose, and if they did see her, could they bring her home."

"Who?" I asked.

"Missy was a cat I had about twenty-five years ago. She was a real sweetheart. But nothing scares a man like a daffy old lady talking about her cats. They cleared out of here quicker than if I'd set the place on fire. How's Mandy?"

"I don't know. I was hoping you knew how to get ahold of her."

"Sorry," said Howard. "She's a good kid. Sharp as a tack. I hope she's all right."

"Me too."

"Do you want some stew?"

"Sure." I'd braced myself for some.

"Me too," said Brian.

"How are the mushrooms?" she asked as she got down a couple of cans of Maggie Dunne.

"Worse than ever," said Brian.

I told her about the green mushrooms and the red mushrooms. She nodded a couple of times.

"So that's what God's wrath is," she said. "My pa never did figure it out."

"Huh?"

"Those red ones," she said. "You said yourself they looked like flames creeping out across the field."

"They do."

"So is devil's fire the blue ones?" Brian asked.

"That's what Pa thought, but he never got the other part straight. He thought the wrath and fire were the same thing. That's why he struggled so much with the story. He knew he had parts of it right, but it came out all wrong. Did you bring that manuscript back?"

"Yeah." I showed her the pages. "I was hoping I could see the rest of it."

"I'm not sure what else there is, but you can poke around while I make stew. You've read that much. You might as well see the rest, if there is any."

I did poke around, and it was easier to do now that all the stories were neatly collated and labeled. There was nothing more about Keatston among the ghastly woodland vapors and sloth monsters in the unpublished works of Max Bailey.

"You saw the mushrooms before, didn't you?" I blurted out once the stew was on the table.

"I was really little at the time, but I saw them," Howard said. "They covered the woods like a blanket but didn't go into town. Pa thought they were fascinating."

"What happened to those mushrooms?" Brian asked. "Did they turn into a monster and then your father killed it?"

She laughed. "It snowed about a foot, and then it got cold. Bitter cold—the kind that takes the skin right off your nose. That put an end to it, but I think Pa was sorry those mushrooms didn't turn into a monster. He wanted to see what they'd do next. He'd heard rumors. . . ." She remembered her stew and ate some, letting her half sentence hang in the air like a ten-day-old helium balloon. "He spent the rest of his life trying to dig up history. What happened to Keatston, and another outbreak in the 1800s nobody ever wrote about, but Pa heard stories from old folks who remembered. That one took a few houses, but nobody was living in them."

"We might lose our house," said Brian. "Dad keeps killing mushrooms, but they keep coming back."

"Pa had pots full of fertilizer and fungi going all over the basement, trying to grow his own monster mushrooms. I moved out as soon as I was old enough. Don't really care to remember him at the end."

"He was a good man," I said. I remembered her saying that.

"He just wanted to do something profound and important," she said. "Nobody took his writing seriously enough. He wanted them to take him seriously. He wanted them to take what he was doing seriously, him and all his friends . . . looking at the edge of the unknown, he would say. It was a good cause, but he wasn't much fun to be around."

I thought about Dad puttering around in the basement with his guitar. I glanced at Brian and guessed he was thinking about the same thing.

"Pa said that science would always outdo the imagination," said Howard. "The mushrooms were proof of it— something scarier than any made-up monster, but real. His masterpiece was going to be a work of science and history, he said. A nonfiction horror story."

"I like the part I read," I said. "I don't know how true it is, though."

"Probably not very," said Howard. "Pa was mixed up about the fire and the wrath. What else does that picture say?"

"'The seeds of redemption are in the people,'" said

Brian. I wondered if he was the smart kid in his class who knew all the answers. "It says that the devil's fire may burn again and that God's wrath will purify the earth and the seeds of redemption are in the people."

"Well, there you go," she said. "Pa thought the green ones might have turned red if they'd gotten the chance. He never got that there were good ones and bad ones. The devil's fire and God's wrath."

"Good mushrooms and bad mushrooms?"

"It's a dog-eat-dog world," she said. "There are bugs that eat other bugs and fish that eat other fish. Why not mushrooms that eat other mushrooms?"

"You mean fungi that eat other fungi," I said.

"The red ones are all around the Meetinghouse," said Brian. We both looked at him. "In the picture at the museum," he explained. "The red ones are all around it like it's burning up, but that's the building that survived."

"That's it," said Howard. "I don't know how Pa never saw it. I think the faster you grow them red ones, the better."

"But how do we do that?" I asked.

"Maybe we can take some from the football field and spread them around," said Brian.

"Hm." I thought it over. The caps did make spores, but did they do it right away? Even if they did, how could you get spores to turn into mushrooms?

On the way back Brian and I biked over to the football field and tested a few red mushrooms. They seemed less sturdy than the green ones; the caps came off easily. I rolled one in my hands until it disintegrated, but I couldn't figure out if there were spores in there I could spread around. I remembered Mandy's story about pigs eating the caps. But who knew if these were safe for a pig to eat?

"Maybe you can buy packs of them, like you do with seeds," Brian said.

"Maybe," I agreed, although I didn't think we'd ever find these particular mushrooms, even if they did sell packets of mushroom spores.

"How did they do it?" Brian asked.

"How did who do it?"

"The Keatston people," he said. "Somebody must have planted the red ones if they made a picture to tell us what to do."

"Tell us what to do?" I'd always seen the picture as a historical depiction, not instructions. I suddenly wanted to see it again, looking at it the right way.

There was only one way to do it. I had to go to the place in Maine where I was least welcome. I went after school on Monday. It was November now, and the Meetinghouse was converted back into a museum.

The woman at the door held up a long purple fingernail to stop me. I recognized her as the not-very-scary witch from this year's haunted house. I think she recognized me, too. They must have had a picture of me taped up somewhere.

"Just one second," she said. "Mr. Ritter?" she called.

Mr. Ritter appeared from the back room, nodding in recognition as soon as he saw me. I knew him, too. He usually did the lecture and tour when we came here on school visits.

"I'm afraid we'll have to ask you to leave," he said. The woman could have told me that, but she must have wanted backup. "I think you'll appreciate why?" He was soft-spoken, just like he was when he was leading fourth graders past the museum cases.

"I just wanted to look at the picture of Keatston," I said. "Maybe ask a couple of questions?"

The woman with the purple nails shot a look at Mr. Ritter.

"It's fine," he said. "I'll keep an eye on him." He reached out and ushered me over to the picture, which was still hanging in the back room. I murmured the words to myself: "'The devil's fire may burn again. God's wrath will purify the earth. The seeds of redemption are in the people.'" They were *instructions*. I knew what the first two parts meant, but what did the last part mean?

"You said you had questions," Mr. Ritter said, glancing at his watch.

"What does that writing mean?"

"It's typical for the period," Mr. Ritter said. "The Great Awakening had its share of poets and prophets. Jonathan Edwards had his 'Sinners in the hands of an angry god.' George Whitefield had his 'Come, poor, lost, undone sinner, come just as you are.' You had to turn a phrase if you wanted to attract a congregation."

I took that to mean that Mr. Ritter didn't understand the writing any more than I did.

"Nobody knows who did this picture?" I asked, grasping for things to ask.

"No," he agreed. "It may not have even been done by a person in Keatston, though it certainly dates from the pre-Revolutionary period."

"And nobody survived?"

"It's hard to say. Nobody *remained*," he said. "People may have scattered to other towns, or moved back to Boston, but there's no record of what happened. You have to understand that those were turbulent days. There was an epidemic of smallpox, and then the war. . . ."

I remembered what Mandy had said to ask.

"How come the Meetinghouse survived and nothing else did?"

"That's an excellent question," he said. "It seems to be at the center of the conflagration, doesn't it? I suppose the reproduction emphasizes the miracle of its escape. As if divine power had spared it, and the pure of spirit . . ." He trailed off. "Well, the truth may be less miraculous. The blaze probably began among the cluster of houses and simply didn't touch the Meetinghouse. The picture may not be that faithful to the facts. Any other questions? I really should return to my duties, and I'm afraid I can't leave you unattended."

I wished I had Mandy with me. She would have known what else to ask. I scanned the picture, afraid to ask the man if the licks of flame looked rather like mushroom caps (which they did), but hoping to find another clue. Or at least stall for time.

248

"Who's the boy in the window?" The question came out of nowhere. I just noticed him again, looking back at us with wide eyes. Everybody else in the picture was running around looking at the fire. Only the boy was looking back at us, and I suddenly had a strong feeling about him.

"We certainly don't know that," he said. "Although there are surviving records documenting the residents of Keatston, there were a dozen boys and young men. Not that the figure has to be a specific person. The artist could have been re-creating a scene he or she only imagined and did not witness firsthand." .

"I bet that's the artist," I said. "Why else would he be looking back at us?"

Mr. Ritter leaned in to squint at the boy. "That's a really interesting theory," he said. "Of course there's no way to ascertain that now. Absent a mark of any kind that identifies the artist . . ."

"What if that *is* his mark? He put himself dead center because it's a self-portrait."

"It's an astounding thought," he said.

I realized why the boy looked familiar. Now the cords were exposed and I could see how everything connected: the seeds of redemption were in the people.

I took the path to Michelle's that night, stopping as soon as I was at the gate to remove the carving of William Keats from my pocket—I'd decided it had to be him. I glanced around and saw a flicker of a curtain at the back window. Michelle knew I was here.

I twisted the preacher's head until it snapped off, spilling some powder onto the back of my hand and my sleeve. I hadn't thought to bring gloves. I brushed my hands off over the compost and tapped the rest of the spores out of the carving like I was peppering a steak. That was all there was to the planting. I looked at the compost heap for a while and realized that nothing would grow while I watched.

I'd looked it up on the Internet and found out that some fungi are capable of wiping each other out—farmers and gardeners will do it sometimes. It was enough to convince me I was on the right track. The red mushrooms were the good guys.

When I turned again, Michelle was waiting on the back porch, holding the door open. She waved at me, and I waved back before I went over. Once again I had lots of explaining to do.

The next day the compost heap had a sprinkling of red in it, and by afternoon it looked like it was burning up. I felt a glimmer of hope. A couple of days later they poured straight from the heap and into the woods. This fungus spread even faster than the first one, the core planted in the nourishing mushroom paradise of a dung heap.

Cassie was anxious, trotting up and down the length of her sty, grumbling and snorting. She'd never been worked up about the blue-green ones, but she hated the red ones.

"What's this supposed to do?" Michelle asked.

"Purify the earth," I told her.

"Hm. Hardly worth it if it upsets a pig."

250

She couldn't argue with the results, though. The devil's fire—as I'd come to think of the first fungus—was nearly wiped out of the field, and in the woods it was fading and creeping back. Instead of working itself up to blasting a billion trumpets and climbing out of the earth, the evil fungus was in retreat.

At night there was rumbling from the woods, and the flashing and clashing of red and blue-green lights. I watched from my window, pangs of fear and excitement rippling through my body. Police cars and fire trucks lined the street, and men and women with floodlights and protective uniforms traveled by twos and threes into the woods, only to come out again scratching their heads.

"No fire! Just fireworks!" one of them shouted to the neighbors who'd gathered in their backyards.

A lot of people packed their cars and left. Tom's family was among them.

"My mom has a really bad feeling about all this," he told me. "We're going to my aunt's place in Concord."

"For how long?"

"However long it takes," he said. "You guys be safe."

"What do you think is going to happen?"

"My mom has a really bad feeling about all this," he said.

By Thursday morning the devil's fire had pulled all its soldiers from our yard, the red fungus giving chase. Mr. Davis stumbled out in his own yard in his pajamas and slippers, falling to his knees and blessing the ruined lawn. On the other side, Sparky ran along the back fence, barking jubilantly.

As dusk fell on Friday, there was howling and shrieking from the woods. The trees shook as if they were in a high wind. Our house seemed to rattle. The plaster on the ceiling cracked and white dust snowed onto the carpets. Through the back door I could see the shed collapse, the wood already weakened by the fungus.

"Maybe we should go," Mom said.

"You're not supposed to drive in an earthquake," said Dad.

"I don't think it's an earthquake," I said.

"Anyway, you're not supposed to drive."

He made us crouch on the floor in the family room, everybody behind a piece of furniture. "My buddy in L.A. told me to do this," he explained. The house shook again, and there was another shower of plaster.

Then the screaming started. The mushrooms had screamed before like warriors rushing into battle. Now they screamed like warriors being vanquished—the combination of the noise and the shaking made me think my whole body would come apart at the seams.

"I'm scared!" Brian shouted.

I put my arm around him, and Dad put his arm around me, and we lay there in a huddled mass while the house shook and the screaming went on and on. Mom was across the room, behind an armchair. I slipped out and crawled over there so she wouldn't be alone.

"Thanks," she said, clutching my hand.

It was like that all night. We lost electricity and heard a horrible noise that turned out to be part of the garage collapsing on Dad's car, but the house held up.

It was still dark when it finally grew quiet and still. Mom had fallen asleep on my shoulder.

"You awake?" Dad whispered.

"Yeah. But I'm trapped."

"Here." He crept over and handed me a sofa cushion. I slid it between Mom's head and the back of the chair so I could get out without waking her.

"I'm going to go look," said Dad.

I got up and followed him to the back door. He stopped cold, then stepped out of the way so I could see.

An enormous black bear was in the backyard, running in a slow and uneven circle around the ruined shed. I could see it in the moonlight. That was all there was. The electricity was out, and there was no mushroom light anymore. The bear tried to scramble up the dead trees and lost its footing, roared, and waved its paws, then went back the other way and disappeared into the woods.

"That was amazing," said Dad.

"Yeah," I agreed. I hoped the bear would gallop up to Michelle's house so she could get a few pictures.

We stood there looking, even though there was nothing to see. The woods were completely dark. The wrath of God had purified the woods.

Chapter 28 AGAINST THE RAZOR RULE

The news called it an ordinary earthquake, even though there are never earthquakes in Maine. Not *real* earthquakes, where the earth moves all on its own. It was the easiest story to tell. Since the news about the Foxfire Festival, there had been a lot of talk about things happening in threes: a fungus, a riot, and an earthquake. There were also jokes that it was just the beginning, that next it would rain frogs or something.

I had to stop listening. Nobody was telling the truth. They wanted to explain it all away.

On the upside, the museum decided not to prosecute me for breaking and entering. In fact, I was made an honorary member after I led Mr. Ritter to the cabin in the woods. It was a treasure trove for museum people—two dozen more carvings and old tools belonging to the hermit who had lived there.

Mr. Ritter wept when he saw the original engraving used to make the print of Keatston. It was on the floor in a pile of dust, the wood blackened with age and ink.

"It's cast aside like garbage," he said, running his hand over the engraving. "But it's astonishing how well it's held up."

I noticed two jutting stones on the wall and guessed what had really happened—the carving had been turned into a shelf, and I'd knocked it off the wall when I was stumbling around in the dark.

"I think it was Benjamin Keats who lived here," I told him.

"From what we know, he was banished for fighting. So it would make sense if he was living like a hermit."

"Maybe they were wrong about him," I said. I didn't really know any better, but I felt like defending old Ben.

"The town of Keatston kept excellent records, and one of the last entries says William threw out his own son for using a knife on people."

"Maybe you're reading it wrong," I said. "I think he liked to carve people. He *whittled*."

"Hm." He saw the tools and the carvings, picked up one, and inspected it. It was a squirrel, both life-sized and lifelike. "So you suppose he was exiled for breaking the second commandment?"

"I don't know." What was the second commandment? "I just think he was a good guy. Maybe he did get into some fights or something, but I don't think he was completely evil."

"It's an intriguing idea," said Mr. Ritter.

"I know it's against that razor rule," I said. "Our science teacher told us the simplest explanation is supposed to be the right one."

"History is the opposite," he said. "No matter how you explain something, the truth is always more complicated."

I did have to do some community service for assault with a deadly pumpkin, because the cops didn't drop their own charges. I'd be picking up litter along the highway. Things could have ended up a lot worse.

The Saturday after Thanksgiving I biked to Boise Township. I took the highway instead of the trail. The grass off to the side was white with frost. I wondered if that would have killed the fungus anyway. Maybe, but who knows what the fungus would have done in the meantime. I added that to a mental list of questions that I might never know the answers to.

I was sure the cabin in the woods was Ben's, and that he'd discovered the red mushrooms, and that he'd scattered their spores around the Meetinghouse to fight the devil fungus. Later—I don't know how much later, or what happened in between—he made the prints with instructions on what to do if the devil's fire came back. He might have made dozens, but only one survived. He'd put the spores into the carvings, probably because they already existed. Maybe he felt like he was running out of time. He never would have guessed that he'd be helping people in the twenty-first century.

That was a lot of speculation, and I was going to learn everything I could to find out whether any of it was true.

I'd never been to Randy's house before, and I was surprised to see his room. There was practically no football stuff. He had a lot of books and freaky-looking posters with drooling monsters. I recognized a couple as prints of Max Bailey paintings.

"So what's up?" he asked me.

"I was, uh . . . You know, you post sometimes on this Internet message board for sci-fi geeks. I mean sci-fi fans."

"I use more than one," he admitted. "Which one?"

"It was for Max Bailey fans," I told him, "and you posted a picture of the glowing mushrooms before they were a big deal."

"Yeah, when you showed me those mushrooms, I thought, Man, the guys on the Miskatonic Web are going to love this. So I took a picture with my phone and posted it when I got home."

"Misawhat?"

"Miskatonic Web. It's what that board is called."

"Anyway, this girl asked you about the picture. I was hoping her profile had an email address or something."

I was worried that he'd give me a bunch of "Ooh, you have a girlfriend" nonsense, but he didn't. He opened a laptop and brought up the message board in a second, then paged back through the threads for a while. "Lots of activity on this site," he explained. He finally found it and clicked it, skimmed through.

"Is her name Mary?" he asked me.

"Huh?"

"Her user name is Mary K. Like the makeup company."

"Mary Killer," I said. "The K is for Killer."

He clicked the name and shook his head. "Email is hidden. I can send a personal message, but she'll have to log in to see it. And this says she hasn't been on in six weeks, so she might not see it for a while."

"Crud." Whatever school she was at now must not let

students use the Internet. I did know she wasn't at Alden anymore, but that was all Mom would tell me. Not if she'd been expelled or yanked out by her parents, and definitely not her contact info. I didn't even know where Mandy was from—maybe the Midwest, from the way she talked, but that was all I knew. I'd searched MySpace and Facebook, but there were a gazillion girls named Amanda Morris or Mandy Morris. She might try to find me, too, but there were a lot of guys named Eric Parrish, too. I'd searched once.

"You like this girl?" he asked. He wasn't teasing me, just asking.

"She's a friend," I said. I hadn't really thought about smoochy-type liking with any girl, but I did like hanging out with Mandy. I wanted to tell her everything I'd learned. Maybe just because she would think it was interesting and halfway believe me.

"I'll PM her anyway," said Randy. "Should I give her your phone number?"

"Sure."

Randy typed for a few seconds and hit return. So that was that, but I could have asked him over the phone. It wasn't the only reason I was here.

"I heard about your leg knitting up funny," I blurted. "Will told me. I'm really sorry, Randy."

"It might not be a big deal," he said. "Maybe it will be. I don't know yet. I know I can't play next year, but maybe the year after that."

"But if you miss next year, it'll be harder to get scholarships to one of those prep schools, and if you go to

Hamlin High, it'll be harder to get scouted for college." I'd thought about it the way he must be thinking about it. "You had it all planned out, and I ruined it."

"Ah, I'll figure out another way to get to the NFL," he said. "And if I don't, I'll come up with something else to dream about."

I had a thought, which meant cycling home on the icy trail through the woods. I went off the trail near Alden and left my bike, stamping through the frost until I found the spout of the old sewer pipe.

It had been capped, a formidable lid of metal welded on the end. Somewhere back there, Mandy's phone was still lying broken and lifeless. I might have been able to resurrect it enough to get in touch with her, but it was another dead end.

When I got home, Dad was strumming on his guitar and humming to himself. He still hadn't moved back to Boston because his car was wrecked. He was taking his time about getting a new one. Brian was on the couch, watching and listening.

"Working on the movie song?" I asked him.

"Yep. I haven't written a new song in ages," he said. "I'm kind of rusty." He strummed again and mumbled some nonsense words.

Dad's band got a lot of exposure from the national news. Some clips of the concert got onto YouTube and got about a million hits each. Then folks figured out that the Bright Fun Guys were really Arkham Hat Shop, and their stuff started to sell like crazy on used-CD websites. A music company called them about putting out a greatest hits album and getting their backlist on iTunes. Then a big-time director wanted a song for a sound track to a movie based on the Gninjas video game. Brian practically turned himself inside out from excitement when he got the news.

All of that took precedence over Dad getting a new car or moving back to the city.

He strummed, tightened a peg, and strummed again.

"I don't even know what a Gninja is. What do they do?"

"They kill bugs and save the world," said Brian.

"They kill bugs and save the world," Dad sang. "They slash their swords at insects, too. Who can the brave gnome ninjas be?"

I realized he was playing the chords to "Don Quixote."

"I like it," I told him.

"I bet Gordon Lightfoot's lawyers would like it too," he said. "I got nothing else."

"When are we moving to Boston?" Brian asked out of nowhere.

"What?" Dad looked at him. "Oh, yeah, well . . . We have to talk, because, you know, the house does need work, but I got kind of tied up with stuff and I lost my job down there anyway and, well, we're talking about L.A. There's a talk show that wants us on, and the album to mix, and . . ."

"You said I couldn't go to the set of the movie and now *you're* going?" Brian said.

"I said there is no set because it's animated, and I'm *not* going, I'm just going to—"

Brian stormed up the stairs before Dad could finish the sentence.

"You're moving to California?" I asked.

"I'm going to California, but it's not definitely a move yet."

"What about us?"

"It's just . . . It's like if the New England Patriots called you and asked you to be in the Super Bowl, Eric. What would you do?"

"I don't have children," I reminded him.

"Ouch. Wow, that really . . . Ouch." He patted his chest to show me where it hurt.

I headed up the stairs after Brian. The truth was I didn't want to go anywhere, anyway. Forget the Patriots. I wanted to stay in Tanglewood. My only dream was for things to stay the way they were. The sad thing was I probably had a better chance of getting that call from Bill Belichick.

Brian was on his bed with Digger and Starling, watching them waddle around on the comforter. The spongy terrain was freaking them out a little bit, and they were taking tiny, tentative steps, trying to figure out why the world had gone soft beneath them. I knew how they felt.

Brian had been spending more time in his room since Allan moved away. I noticed he had a tin can on his dresser, filled with drying caps of the red fungus. He must be harvesting the spores. He was thinking ahead. There was also some wood glue from Dad's workshop sitting there, and the carving of Ben—I was now sure it was Ben—with his head back in place. It wasn't good as new, but it was close.

"Hey," he said. His eyes were rimmed with red, but he didn't sound angry.

"How're you doing, buddy?"

"Terrible." He reached out to nudge one of the hedgehogs, who was close to the edge of the bed. She turned and headed back toward the middle.

"Remember how you said I could punch you?"

"Yeah." Maybe it was a dumb thing to offer.

"Can I punch Dad instead?"

"Ha. I don't think so. It wouldn't make you feel better anyway."

"Let me try," he said.

"I know you're mad about Dad leaving," I said. "I am too. But we can't really do anything to make him stay. Making music is what Dad does. He has to do it, like the hedgehogs have to eat bugs."

Brian sniffed.

"It'll be all right," I told him.

"You don't know that," he said.

"I guess not," I admitted.

"Can we go bug hunting tomorrow?" he asked.

There'd been a frost and bugs would be hard to find. On the other hand, it was something Brian wanted to do.

"Sure thing."

The phone rang a bit later, and Dad hollered my name from downstairs instead of carrying the phone up. "It's a girl!" he shouted.

I sprinted down the hall to pick up the extension in my

parents' room. My mom's room, I mean. Dad was sleeping on the couch these days.

The caller ID said B. Morris in Edina, Minnesota.

"Hello? Mandy?"

"So I am strictly forbidden to use the computer right now, but everybody went to the megamall to go shopping. I was supposed to go with, but I pretended to have food poisoning, which I practically do, because they let my big sister help with dinner. Anyway, I got your message. So hi."

"Hi. Uh . . ." I didn't want to jump in by talking about battling fungi and lost history. I needed to make small talk and work my way up to it. "You live in Minnesota?"

"Yeah. I'm even staying. I got into this alternative school in Minneapolis for messed-up goth kids that's close to the U. It should be all right for a while." She told me a bit more about the school. Kids could design their own schedules and even sign up for college classes with special permission. She was going to take a class on early-American literature. "Some of it's really boring but some of it's awesome," she said. "Like Irving and Poe."

"That sounds awesome," I said. It probably was for her. "No Max Bailey?"

"He's not that early, but maybe I can do that next," she said. "I can't wait to tell the teacher I kind of know his daughter."

"And found his long-lost manuscripts," I added.

"I practically lived one of his stories," she said with a laugh that nearly turned into a sob. "What a crazy couple of weeks *that* was."

"You missed the last part," I said. I started to tell her about the seeds of redemption, but she stopped me.

"Oh, crud. That's the garage door. Listen, write it and send it to me, okay? The whole story."

"I'm no writer."

"Do it anyway. And tell Brian to write me." She gave me her email address. "But now I really gotta go!" she said. "Email me! I might not write back right away, but I will eventually!"

I didn't get a chance to ask her what I really wanted to— what exactly happened, and if she remembered it the way I did, and if she'd ever heard of the razor rule.

Brian and I went out the next morning. It was snowy and I knew the bug search was futile, but it was a nice morning to be in the woods. We stopped by the big stone we'd turned over just before discovering the mushrooms.

"Let's put it back the way we found it," said Brian.

"You mean the stone?"

"Yeah," he said. "We should put things back the way we found them." He reached into his pocket, found something, and set it down in the hollow beneath the rock.

I couldn't see it, but I had an idea of what it was.

Before I could offer to help, Brian walked around the stone and gave it a big shove. It rolled over, sending up a puff of snow.

"Let's go," he said.

We pressed on deeper into the woods.

ACKNOWLEDGMENTS

For the third time, I give grateful acknowledgment to Angela Scaletta, Tina Wexler, and Allison Wortche for their feedback and enthusiasm through the writing and revision process. Thanks to Sarah Hokanson, Kathleen Dunn, and the rest of the team at Random House Children's Books. Lots of gratitude and shellfish to The Otters for their advice and input: Josh Berk, Steve Brezenoff, Jonathan Roth, and Jon Skovron. Laurel Snyder and Linda Joy Singleton were way beyond helpful in the planning phase. Much of the bullying subplot was enriched by the thoughtful writing and friendship of James Preller. Charlotte the cat and her favorite toy inspired the Cassie story. Sy Montgomery's lovely memoir, *The Good Good Pig*, told me everything I needed to know about having a pet pig. H. P. Lovecraft inspired the character and imaginary oeuvre of Max Bailey. Elaine Ford brought me to Maine in the first place and is the best writing teacher I ever had. A minor remembrance of a Mainer friend, Jennifer McLeod Finch, is now part of Eric's story. Max Kimball was the first kid who read this story and liked all the parts I hoped he would. I brainstormed titles with the kids in Guys Read at Rockford Road in Crystal, Minnesota (special thanks to Zack), and got advice from the kids at South View Middle School in Edina, Minnesota, the kids at St. Michael-Albertville Middle School in St. Michael, Minnesota, and the kids at St. Joseph's School in Menomonie, Wisconsin. Byron Ely Scaletta *is,* and that's all I ask of him.

ABOUT THE AUTHOR

Kurtis Scaletta was born in Louisiana and grew up in New Mexico, North Dakota, England, Liberia, Brazil, and a few other places. His books for young readers include *Mudville,* which was a *Booklist* Top 10 Sports Book for Youth, and *Mamba Point,* which the *New York Times Book Review* called "entertaining and touching."

Kurtis now lives in Minneapolis with his wife, their son, and several cats. To learn more about him and his books, please visit kurtisscaletta.com.